THE FIRE OPAL

ALSO BY REGINA MCBRIDE

The Marriage Bed
The Land of Women
The Nature of Water and Air

The FIRE OPAL

REGINA McBRIDE

DELACORTE PRESS

Delacorte Press is a registered trademark and the colophon is a trademark of Random House, Inc.

Visit us on the Web! www.randomhouse.com/teens
Educators and librarians, for a variety of teaching tools, visit us at
www.randomhouse.com/teachers

Library of Congress Cataloging-in-Publication Data
McBride, Regina.
The fire opal / Regina McBride.—1st ed.
p.   cm.
Summary: While invading English soldiers do battle in sixteenth-century Ireland, Maeve grows up with a mystical connection to a queen who, centuries before, faced enemies of her own, and uses her special gifts to try to save her mother whose spirit has left her.
ISBN 978-0-385-73781-4 (hc)—ISBN 978-0-385-90692-0 (glb)—
ISBN 978-0-375-89544-9 (e-book)
[1. Supernatural—Fiction.   2. Family life—Ireland—Fiction.   3. Mythology, Celtic—Fiction.   4. Ireland—History—1558–1603—Fiction.]   I. Title.
PZ7.M478274Fir 2010
[Fic]—dc22   2009007573

The text of this book is set in 12-point Horley Old Style.
Book design by Trish Parcell Watts
Printed in the United States of America
10 9 8 7 6 5 4 3 2 1
First Edition

For Miranda, with love

CONTENTS

WESTERN COAST OF IRELAND

COUNTY DONEGAL

Late Sixteenth Century

PROLOGUE

When I was seven years old, my mother and I spent a July afternoon on the foreshore collecting kelp, which we planned to dry and burn for summer fires. It was a rare sunny day, the light blinding on the tide.

On our way home, we reached the old ruins, a great edifice with towers, now roofless, and long since crumbled in the harsh salt wind. My brothers and I often played here, exploring and hiding among its walls and foundation stones.

Mam's creel basket was so heavy she put it down and sat on the broken stone stairway of the ruin, where sea grass and maidenhair ferns grew through the cracks.

She gazed out at the waves and the horizon, a faraway look on her face. Now and again that day, as we'd been gathering, I'd seen her lost in her thoughts, staring past the sea with this same earnest, distracted expression. I ached to know what she was thinking about, and now I asked her.

"I don't really know that I can explain it, Maeve," she said.

"Try, Mam," I said.

"When I look at the horizon, I feel"—she paused, searching for the right words—"a yearning for something, but I don't know what it is."

She looked back at the horizon, and the same expression softened her features. She seemed so separate from me in that moment that it made me uneasy.

"What could it be you're yearning for, Mam?" I asked, and touched her arm to bring her back.

She shook her head vaguely.

"Is it something you lost?" I asked.

"Maybe." She smiled. "Something I lost long ago, before I was born."

I stared out to where she was staring, hungry to understand. And that was when I heard a phrase of elusive music that dissolved when I strained to hear it better.

"Mam," I said. "Did you hear music?"

She looked surprised by the question. "No," she said. She got to her feet, picking up her heavy basket, and added, "Let's go home now."

Later that afternoon, after helping Mam lay out the kelp to dry, I went back down to the ruins to see if I could hear the music again. Just as I was beginning to focus on the horizon, a tide rushed high onto the beach with unusual force, reaching me and surrounding my ankles, pulling me so that I fell in the sand. When the tide withdrew, it left a great heap of kelp. Immediately I thought how pleased Mam would be if I gathered as much as I could and brought it home to dry with the rest. As I did, I spied an object, tangled in the vines and leaves. It was about six feet long and looked to be made of iron and other wrought metals inlaid with veined stone.

I squatted down and gingerly swept ribbons of obscuring kelp away from it to get a better look. Decoratively engraved all over it were swirling symbols and animals with fierce faces and open mouths breathing fire. Embellished with leaves and fruits were the words THE ANSWERER.

I saw that there had once been a sharp spear at the top, but most of it was now broken jaggedly away. Maybe it had served as a weapon for a giant. Only the elaborate handle was still well intact, though rusted and barnacled as if it had spent centuries on the seafloor.

It was very heavy, and it took all my strength to turn it over. The other side was different. The carvings formed a kind of face with stylized features and a single swirling eyebrow over a large jewel eye—a kind of Cyclops. The jewel was both transparent and dim, with rich purple and brownish depths.

As I was gazing into it, a dark embankment of clouds moved in and obscured the sun. I heard my brothers' voices on the hill above and panicked, feeling intensely possessive of this extraordinary object. I knew if they saw it they would take it. The two of them would be strong enough to lift it, and their games with it would be rough. They'd damage it or lose it somewhere.

Hoping they wouldn't see, I struggled to place the object

back in the kelp, and inadvertently kicked a stone loose near a ruined pedestal. Turning, I noticed an opening under the broken stair. I knelt down and looked in, surprised to see a very low collapsed-earth room, in places only about four feet from the ceiling to the floor. It seemed a perfect spot to hide this object.

As I pushed it with great effort, sliding it toward the opening under the stair, I felt a warmth under my hands and saw a shadow move along the surface of the jewel eye. I felt certain that the thing was looking at me.

As the object fell onto the soft ground in the ruined room, I was sure I heard it moan and sigh, as if in relief. I lay there on my belly looking through the opening. "The Answerer," I whispered, wondering over the name. It sank slightly into the loamy earth.

I was about to cover the opening up with stones when it began to rain, and my brothers' voices faded into the distance. They had not even seen me down here. With no urgency now to hide my find, I remained there lying on my stomach looking in.

I decided that I would try to get the object out again, but a shower of mysterious red sparks fell from the low ceiling in the underground room and floated down over the Answerer, settling into the grooves of its embellishments.

Farther back in the shadows, I noticed a kind of shelf or dresser, now collapsed. It appeared to be composed of white stone with a green matrix, some kind of marble, perhaps, emblazoned with red stars. Each time bits of light fell from the ceiling, the stars sparked with a red brilliance, and the

Answerer sighed like a sentient being. It seemed to belong here, and that filled me with a mysterious satisfaction. It was meant to be hidden.

Before I left, and as the rain began to deluge me, I covered the opening in the stair with mud and stones.

That night at home, with kelp burning along with the turf, the air in the cottage smelled of the ocean. My head pounded and my face felt hot. Soon I was delirious.

Gripped by a high fever, I had my mother in a terror, thinking I would not survive.

From my sickbed, I saw the Answerer standing upright near the hearth cinders, focused on me with its deep, brimming eye. I sensed that it was grateful to me for concealing it in the hidden room. But it remained by the fire for a long time, gazing across the shadowy, smoky air of the cottage room, as Mam and I had gazed across the sea toward the horizon.

The next morning, my fever broke and I slept all day. I suffered amnesia with regard to the Answerer. I forgot about finding it the day before on the shore and hiding it possessively from my brothers. As if some spell had deprived me of the memory, I forgot I'd lain in the rain shivering because I did not want to take my eyes off it. I remembered it only vaguely as a presence that had stood near my sickbed.

And so it was consigned to the realm of figments and ghosts, the shadows of impossible creatures that live in the feverish imagination of a child.

Seven years later . . .

Part One

*The Coast
of Rain and Shadows*

CHAPTER 1

The March wind was wild that Saturday morning when I left the cottage with my brothers to go down the hill to the beach.

I squinted and yawned in the mild sunlight as we descended from the promontory upon which our cottage sat exposed to the full force of the Atlantic gales. I shivered, pulling close the collar of my oilcloth coat.

None of us had slept well the night before.

Our mam had been up crying, and though our da had done his best to calm her, she'd been restless and uneasy over something particular, something she spoke of only in whispers.

Mam had not been fully herself since tragedy had struck our house the year before, when my baby sister had grown sick and died. Now my brothers and I all wanted to shake off the long sleepless night we'd just passed.

My brother Donal began to race toward the rocks where he saw our da's boat beached. "I'm taking the boat out!" he screamed.

"The wind is too strong!" Fingal called out to him over the noise of the waves. "The boat'll be dashed to the rocks!"

The waves broke and arched up, foaming and falling across the shoals.

"Our vessel can ride those swells!" Donal shouted proudly. He stood near the boat but made no efforts to drag it into the tide. I knew he was just taunting Fingal, who was of a cautious nature. Even Donal, daredevil that he was, wouldn't tempt water so agitated.

My brothers and I had helped our father craft the boat and had lined it threefold in fat sealskins. Mam said that if the boat had a soul, it was a seal's soul, the way it moved, long and dark and sure of itself, cutting the waters. So she had named it *Mananan's Vessel* after the Irish sea god.

"I've an idea," Donal said with a desperate sort of exuberance. "Let's take the boat and leave Ard Macha for good and sail in search of the Holy Isles."

"There's no such place as the Holy Isles," Fingal bellowed over the noise of the surf.

"Many people have reported seeing them," Donal insisted.

"They're imaginary. They're only territories of the mind," Fingal said, the wind blowing so hard it carried his voice above us and sent it seaward.

All my life, I had heard stories about those mysterious isles, where the goddess who had once ruled Ireland had exiled herself in centuries past. Some said the isles lay to the south, and others said they were to be found at a more northerly latitude. They were known by many names— the Holy Isles, the Land of Women, the Country of the Perpetually Young, the Isles of the Dispossessed—and were supposed to be otherworldly places where extraordinary things occurred.

"They have never been mapped or charted," Fingal said, always the one to require proof of things.

Donal and Fingal were fifteen, one year older than I, and though they were twins, they could not have been more different. Donal had dark brown hair like mine and Mam's, and he was strong and solidly built, while Fingal had red hair like our da's and was slender. Donal was fiery and impulsive, while Fingal approached things with logic and caution. I often felt pulled between the two poles of their different natures, but today, Donal's wish to escape resonated strongly with my own feelings.

Though the sun shone weakly through the clouds in the eastern sky, the horizon to the west was all mist. The idea of such an adventure, sailing to the west in search of mystical isles, appealed to me greatly. Mam's unhappiness had been wearing away at my spirit. I ached for the world to open up before me.

"I think it's sad that you don't believe in the Holy Isles, Fingal," Donal said.

Fingal laughed. "I think it's sad that you do!"

"Stop fighting about it," I snapped. "And you both know we can't take the boat out in this weather." The wind intensified, and our coats beat and rippled wildly around us.

I envisioned the three of us in Da's boat, sailing through an otherworldly place, the dark clouds broken and ignited with green glimmering light. The Holy Isles were said to be a province altogether different from ours, lit by a black sun. I imagined the sea and the clouded sky illuminated by a dark planetary brilliance.

My two brothers were restless, full of energy and uncertain what to do with it. They ran closer to the water and began kicking stones, making them skid across the water. I saw Fingal bend down, finding something among the flotsam from the tides; then the two of them came running back.

"Look what I found, Maeve." Fingal held up a jagged piece of something shiny. "A mirror. There's enough sunlight that I can start a little fire with it."

The three of us squatted down near a clump of beach grass.

"You see, you get the sunlight in the mirror," he said, angling it back and forth with blinding flashes, "and shine it on the grass."

We formed a kind of wall around the grass, blocking the wind. Fingal moved the mirror very carefully, and a blade of grass began to burn; soon, two other blades near it caught on fire.

A sudden loud commotion of birds sounded from the estuary around the rocks to the north. Gulls circled overhead, screeching wildly. As we stood, the wind put out our little fire.

We ran toward the noise, balancing precariously on the stones and leaning against the rock wall, making our way to the estuary. Tom Cavan, a boy a year older than my brothers who lived in the cottage closest to ours on Ard Macha and whom we'd known and disliked all our lives, was clutching tightly to a bit of slippery cliff shelf, stuck there, not certain how to get down safely. A large gull swept back and forth past him, its beak open, threatening to bite. That was when I noticed the hatchlings that lay dead below on the stones.

I pointed them out to my brothers.

"You devil! You lout!" Donal yelled at him.

"Help me, O'Tullagh!" Tom cried. "One of you climb over and around the other way and give me a hand up."

"No! You monster!" Donal yelled.

"You're getting your due! I hope she plucks your eyes out!" Fingal said.

"And why do you care so much about these nuisance birds?" Tom asked.

One of the hatchlings squirmed and moved its hardly formed wing.

"Fingal," I said, touching my brother's arm. "One of them is alive."

He went over to it and squatted beside it. "The poor creature is still breathing," he said, and lifted it very carefully, holding it in one cupped hand.

"I don't think it's long for this world," Donal remarked, looking closely at it.

I touched the hatchling gingerly with one finger, and it blinked and gave a little spasm. Sensing its suffering, I went mad with anger at Tom.

"If it wouldn't make me as low a creature as you, I'd pick up a stone and throw it at you!" I shrieked, trembling so I could barely control myself.

Tom turned his windburned face in my direction, wearing an expression I'd often seen come into his eyes: a cool fascination, almost as if it entertained him to see how outraged he could make me. At such moments, he seemed indifferent to my brothers' anger with him. It was my reaction to his cruelty, my frustration with him, that he seemed to revel in. His green eyes glinted with a spark of orange as he stared at me.

For as long as we could remember, Tom Cavan had gone wild each spring, dropping the eggs of gulls from cliff rocks or throwing new hatchlings from their nests. And he shot down birds he never intended to eat. My brothers and I policed him. Da had said that Tom would likely grow out of that bad behavior, but now Tom was sixteen and seemed worse than ever.

It was a constant source of shock to me that the three girls our age who lived in the nearby valley were all completely smitten with Tom and professed to be jealous that his cottage was so close to mine. They found my contempt for him as incomprehensible as I found their feelings for him. None seemed remotely moved to change her opinion when I explained the cruelty he was capable of. Each shrugged it off as something boys did.

Tom lost his precarious hold on the side of the cliff and fell down about seven feet to the rocks. He winced, probably having hurt his hip bone, but managed to get up, slipping once or twice. His only way out of the estuary was to come past where we stood. Fingal handed me the injured hatchling.

Donal and Fingal grabbed Tom by the shirt and dragged him over the rocks and back toward the beach.

"I hate you, Tom Cavan!" I said, turning away so that I wouldn't have to see his face anymore.

"He's got his slingshot, too." Donal pulled it from Tom's pocket and threw it into the sea. "He's likely been shooting birds as well as knocking them from their nests."

"We're telling your da what you've done!" Fingal cried.

I stayed behind, struggling to catch my breath. I wondered what to do with the poor hatchling. I knew that once a baby bird had fallen from the nest, the mother and father would not accept it back. I decided I would take it home, and was about to when it shivered convulsively and the life went out of it. My face burned hot in spite of the wind, and tears began to flow.

I laid the creature next to its dead siblings and knelt down near them.

The wind came up high. The sky darkened, and a belt

of rain moved in suddenly, bringing with it a procession of squalls. The water came so far inland that it drenched my skirts to the knee and swept over the baby birds, washing them into the sea. For a few moments they bobbed on the back of a wave, and then disappeared.

Back on the higher beach, I looked up toward the cottage, and though the rain began to soak me, I did not want to go home. It seemed to me that things were much too slow to change here on Ard Macha. My mother's unhappiness would not lighten. And Tom Cavan had never learned his lesson, only become increasingly wayward, untrustworthy and cruel.

But it was something else, something I had heard Da say to Fingal quietly by the fire the night before, that made me not want to go home. He'd said that he was afraid for our mam, that the grief over losing little Ishleen had been too much for her, and he feared that her mind was no longer right.

I looked again into the mist on the horizon and felt a palpitating longing to be sailing away in search of mystical isles.

CHAPTER 2

The rain intensified. I pulled my coat close around me, pushing against the wind, and ran north toward the ruins. Centuries of towering waves had eaten it down to natural terraces of rock, and the banisters to pedestals, crumbled and beaten, washed white and broken by the tides. Still, in spite of all the diminishment, there remained a sense of immensity about the place.

We had been told that it had once been a convent for the pious, cloistered order of Saint Brigid. I always doubted that, long before my mother suggested to me that it wasn't true. The nuns I'd seen in the village of Kilcoyle were a meek and retiring lot, and this had once been too powerful and ostentatious a building to house such creatures.

I ran toward a decrepit tower to take shelter from the downpour.

From this spot, looking through the break in the wall, I could see the bog where the men of Ard Macha cut turf for burning. It looked desolate now in the rain, and as I stared, I relived the day last year, also in the month of March, when my baby sister, Ishleen, had become ill.

My da, my brothers, Tom Cavan, and his father, Michael Cavan, had been standing in the bog, cutting the dark loamy earth into neat slices that they'd piled on the ground to dry. Mam and I had brought an afternoon meal to the men. Since she'd been carrying Ishleen at the time, I had held the basket of bread and cheese and the flask of hot tea.

Ishleen had reached and flexed one of her small plump hands toward me and smiled from over Mam's shoulder. I had made a face at her and she'd laughed, her cheeks round and ruddy.

Tom's shovel had hit something hard in the rich uncut ground. As my brothers had been helping him unearth the obstruction, a rancid smell had risen out of the bog. We had all covered our faces in revulsion, but it had caused Ishleen to grow agitated. Mam and I had both spoken softly to her, but she'd begun to kick and squirm in an uncharacteristic way.

The thing that had been unburied was very large, and for a while, no one knew what it was. All five men had gone down on their knees around it, wiping the damp peat away.

"It's armor of some kind," Donal had called out.

Ravens had gathered and sat on the walls of the ruins, facing us. Ishleen's agitation had grown progressively worse, and when my brothers had helped Tom out of the bog hole and onto dry land, Ishleen, her face damp and ablaze, had begun to scream. At a loss, Mam had carried her up the hill, Ishleen's screams echoing down to us.

The thing that had lain under the ground had indeed been armor, as black as pitch from centuries in the bog. It was a piece of back and chest armor, unusual in two shocking ways: it had been made to a woman's form, and the woman who had once worn it had to have been at least ten feet tall, a veritable giantess. Etched into the metal at the shoulders and collar and along the bottom were small images. Fingal had peered closely at these, recoiling now and again at the stench, then touching them with his fingertips to remove any excess turf.

"These are Viking symbols," he'd said, and I'd stepped in to look. The thing had emitted an intense cold.

"I hate to say what I think this is," Fingal had added.

"Tell us," Da had said.

"The armor of a Valkyrie, a Viking corpse goddess. There were battles near here, I heard, seven centuries ago, around the time when the great Brian Boru defeated the Vikings at the battle of Clontarf."

The ravens that had gathered around the ruins had suddenly risen in a noisy panic and flown inland. In the distant sky over the sea, much larger birds were circling, their screeches echoing ominously.

It was the memory of those birds that shocked me back

to the present moment. I sighed. Other than the soft patter of the rain on the bog water, the skies were quiet.

Feeling someone's touch on my shoulder, I gasped and turned. A young woman with dark, agitated eyes stood a few steps behind me, leaning forward from the waist, her arm extended, fingers poised to touch my shoulder again. She wore a cloak, white and very pale gray, and as she slid the hood off her head, bits of goose or swan down drifted from her sleeves.

She cast nervous glances at the bog, and then out at the areas of the hill and beach that could be seen through the break in the tower wall. Undoing the top button of her cloak very deliberately, she revealed a necklace with three faceted crystals, each the size of my thumb, hanging from a silver chain.

With a breathless urgency she detached one of the crystals and said, "Your mother needs this charm. It will protect her."

Looking closely at it, I saw that it was a kind of delicate bottle, containing a disembodied flame.

I wanted to ask many things, but the woman's presence had the effect of silencing me. The ground beneath my feet moved, and my head began to ache, my thoughts unclear. Her urgency seeped into me and she kept speaking in soft, fervent tones, but she seemed to have lapsed into an arcane language, and I could not translate it. I peered at her in great earnestness, as if it were the feelings behind her words, and not the words themselves, that were necessary to absorb.

Though the rain continued to fall, I realized I could no

longer hear it. Nor could I hear the sea, though it had been clearly audible only minutes before. The sky had darkened to a deep blue color, and the entire world seemed to suspend itself in quiet.

The woman was about to go, but she looked at me and hesitated; then she detached another bottle and handed it to me. The flame contained within this one was more robust and brighter red than the other.

I pointed at myself to ask if it was meant for me to keep. She nodded, then stepped away, and I watched her lit figure drift slowly from the ruins. I wanted to follow but could not move from the place where I stood. When I could no longer see her, some spell was broken. I heard the wind again, and the waves.

It stunned me when I realized how dark it was. The rain had stopped. It seemed to me I had spoken to the woman for only a short time, but now evening had come on.

In spite of the desire to reveal everything to Mam, I found myself afraid to. The woman had looked so concerned about Mam. I began concocting a story about how I'd come upon the bottles.

I started home at a quick pace, but stopped in my tracks once to look again at the little bottles. First I looked at the one meant for me. When it caught the light, deep and brilliant colors alternated on its surfaces: emerald into blue, then into violet and a very deep purple. Its beauty filled me with a pleasant sensation and caused my heart to race. I slipped the bottle back into my pocket, then held up the one for Mam in the last of the light, studying it. A symbol was engraved in the metal stopper on top: three spirals, all connected to one another. It was at this moment, while my concentration on the symbol was most intent, that Tom Cavan's voice startled me from close behind.

"What have you got?" he said, and grabbed my arm.

I dropped the bottle and it shattered on the stone, all the liquid within absorbed into the earth.

"Look what you've done!" I screamed. If it had been my bottle broken instead of Mam's, my outrage might have been less.

He stared at me with a smile. "You haven't answered my question. What was that?"

"Nothing at all that is any business of yours, you stupid devil!" I cried, barely containing my rage and disappointment. I squatted down, gathering as quickly as I could the shards and the metal stopper, which had remained intact. He grabbed my hand, laughing as he tried to get the pieces from me. I squeezed so tight that the glass cut my palm numerous times.

At that moment, as blood dripped from my hand and I was nearing the verge of hysteria, I felt a tingling warmth from my skirt pocket. Somehow the sensation of the other bottle there calmed me. I took a deep breath and closed my eyes. While I possess this bottle, I thought, Tom has no power to upset me. When I opened my eyes again, I looked with calm indifference at Tom and saw some confused thought pass over his features, the smile dropping from his face. It was my frustrated anger that he thrived on. I rose to my feet and continued my steady gaze into his eyes.

"I don't believe you have a soul, Tom Cavan," I said with quiet authority.

Irritated by my calm disdain, he looked lost.

Carefully I placed the wet shards and bottle stopper in my other pocket. Tom remained where he was, unmoving, as I took the strip of cloth I used to tie back my hair and wiped the blood from my hand with it. Some of the luminous liquid from the shards had entered the cuts in my palms, causing a pleasant shiver.

I continued on my way home. Gradually, before a full minute had passed, the cuts were gone.

CHAPTER 3

o my great relief, when I got home, Mam did not look upset. She was peeling potatoes, and she gestured with her head to my empty chair next to her, my little peeling knife waiting for me on it. My brothers were sitting near the fire with our father, helping him mend his fishing net.

I smiled at Mam, and she smiled back. I hung up my oilcloth coat at the door and sat down to help her peel.

The kitchen was bright with lamp and firelight. Even when the wind wailed against the outer stones of the cottage, all thatch and mud and whitewash, this room stayed warm. It was the gathering place where everything happened, with its earth floors and open rafters, the walls hung with Mam's dry herbs and Da's fishing tackle, nets and oilskins. The black pot hanging from the crane above the hearth issued the fragrant steam of cooking mackerel.

The rest of the cottage beyond this one area was unlit and plunged in shadow: the box bed with the curtain, where my parents slept, and past that, the narrow winding stair that led to the small loft where my brothers slept. And on the other side, closest to the back door that led directly into the cow byre, my own pallet bed on its curtained platform.

I already felt an intense attachment to this little bottle, the one the woman had said was meant for me, in awe of how it had calmed me and given me authority over Tom! I had been thinking that I'd give it to Mam to replace the broken one, but now I tried to think of ways that I would not have to part with it. Perhaps I could find the woman again and tell her what had happened, and she could spare me the last bottle on the necklace for Mam.

"Where were you?" Donal asked. "We were scouting for you but couldn't find you."

"I waited out the rain in the ruins," I said.

"But where were you after that? It stopped raining ages ago," Da said.

I paused. "Just wandering."

"I suppose the wee bird died," Fingal said.

"Yes," I answered.

"Tom's father is in a fury with him, threatening to send him away from Ard Macha," Donal said.

"But his mam doesn't want him to go, and she's fighting to keep him here though he never lifts a finger to help them," Fingal said.

"He's the last child," Mam said, "and an old cow's calf at that." All of Tom's siblings were much older and had long since scattered to the four winds.

"She's spoiled him, the way she'll never believe a bad thing about him," Da remarked.

"When the Callahan sisters heard that he might leave, they were all in a lather," Donal said.

"Why do those girls fancy him? He's so cruel and awful!"

"Maeve, you're the only girl this side of Killybegs who doesn't melt when she sees Tom Cavan," Donal said.

"Ugh!" I made a repulsed face.

"Don't you see it, Maeve?" Mam asked, looking at me with a gentle curiosity. "Even I see it. He's quite the handsome devil."

"I don't see a handsome devil," I said. "Only a devil."

I was too proud to admit that I had my moments of wonder over Tom's physical beauty. He had high cheekbones, a strong jaw and light brown waves of hair that went gold in the summer. I had only studied him at leisure twice. Both times he had not known that he was being observed, and with no one around to taunt, he'd looked lost in thought and vaguely sad, and I had wondered what it was that drove him to be so malicious.

"I hope he goes soon," I said, excited by the prospect of his disappearing from our lives. "Where might he be sent?"

"I don't know. It isn't for certain yet," Fingal said. "Anyway, enough talk about Tom Cavan." He took out the little notebook in which he liked to chart the stars on clear nights, matching what he saw to the time of year, the month and the day.

At the schoolhouse in Dunloe, Fingal had heard of Galileo and astronomy and had, to no avail, tried to find books in Dungarven or even in the larger port town of Killybegs. He had these notions about the turning of the world and the stars and sun, a desire to somehow see the order in the universe.

But education was difficult to get; teachers passed through, and for long periods of time, there'd be no teacher in residence at all. Because I was a girl, I didn't even have the option of attending. But Donal, who was also a gifted student, taught me to read from a book of adventure tales, a book that was illustrated with etchings of castles and knights and ladies, which he had borrowed from the schoolhouse and intended to return if there was ever a teacher again.

It had been hard lately to get him to read with me, though. He had become preoccupied with fighting the English invaders in Ireland, and collected stories from friends and acquaintances about English atrocities committed against the Irish.

Fingal got up and wandered to the door, looking out and up at the sky. "It'll rain again tonight," he said with disappointment. Rarely was there a night clear enough that Fingal could observe the movements in the heavens. He sat down near the fire with his notebook and began to reread his scribbled observations from the last clear night.

Mam and I were finishing the potatoes, getting ready

to boil them with the mackerel, while Da was stoking the embers, bringing the fire to a roar.

I felt Mam's eyes on me and realized that I kept stopping my knife on the skin of the potato, absorbed by the memory of the woman who had given me the bottles.

"Maeve," Mam said, "are you all right?"

I looked up, startled, wishing I could pour my heart out, but some fear held me back.

"Yes, Mam, I'm fine," I replied, though she continued to look at me doubtfully.

Suddenly Donal spoke. "I heard today about a mother and child that were murdered by English soldiers in Galway."

A shadow fell over Mam's face.

"Donal," I said, and shook my head at him.

He looked at me darkly. "It's all got to be spoken about, Maeve. We cannot pretend it isn't happening."

"All right, then, but don't be so detailed in the way you tell things."

He smoothed back a big lock of dark brown hair that kept falling over one eye. "I'll say only this: the English soldiers value Irish lives less than they value the lives of sheep."

The beautiful little bottle in my pocket seemed to pulse just as Mam looked up from her peelings and announced in a soft voice filled with portent, "I have something to tell you children." Tension filled the air as we all waited, hardly breathing. After a silence, she said, "There's going to be a baby."

We all looked at one another anxiously, but Mam

looked down again at the potato she had in her hands and went quiet.

The rain began to fall, making soft, eerie sounds in the thatch above us.

Mam looked distracted and fragile. When I saw her eyes begin to dampen, I reached with a sudden impulse for the beautiful little bottle in the pocket of my flannel dress and handed it to her.

She put down her knife and took it, holding it up in the firelight.

"How beautiful, Maeve," she whispered, her eyes wide and glistening. "It looks like a little flame in there."

"I found it at the ruins," I said.

Mam gazed at it incredulously. "Is it fire or is it liquid?" she whispered as if to the air. She seemed to forget about the potatoes, her eyes misting over.

"It's for you!" I said suddenly. I felt a physical pain in my stomach at parting with it.

"Thank you, Maeve," she said quietly, tearing her eyes from it to look at me. She reached over with her other hand and brushed the hair from my face. "You've mud in your hair," she said, slightly startled, and smiled. She looked down at my hems and saw mud dried thick there and on my shoes.

I had not noticed a very tiny hole in the top lip of the bottle, but Mam saw it immediately. She put the bottle on a piece of thread and hung it like a necklace around her neck. I thought it astonishing that she knew to wear it as a charm, and this made me ache to tell her about the woman who had also worn it that way. But as Mam picked up her knife again, urging me to do the same, and we peeled the skins from the last of the potatoes, I held back. The woman's concern over Mam caused a heavy weight in my stomach.

When we'd finished, I stoked the fire beneath the pot. Mam suddenly raised her face and listened to something she heard outside. Wiping her hands on a tea towel, she stepped out into the downpour, where she stood without moving.

Da went to her. "Come back inside, Nuala," he said, but she did not reply. After several minutes, each of my brothers chimed in, pleading with her to come inside, but she refused, holding a hand up in the air, still listening hard to something. I went out and stood with her, looking up into her face.

"Do you hear?" she asked me.

At first, I didn't, and I felt my heart growing heavy. But then she took one of my hands in hers, and beyond the drumming and splatter of the rain, I detected another sound. I held my breath and listened to a soft humming, weird and mournful, a voice human-sounding yet hardly human. I recognized it somehow, at moments sweet and plaintive like music, but could not place it. The sound filled me with a vague yearning I could not name. The quiet calling seemed to be coming from everywhere and nowhere at once.

I noticed that the bottle of pale red liquid around Mam's neck wore a kind of aura in the rain, a cape of luminous mist.

The rain silenced a little, and the sound took more

volume. With a shock, I recognized it as the voice of a single swan. Though it was nowhere to be seen, I knew the song to be identical to the cries of the wild swans that sometimes frequented the lake near the bog. I had often heard them sing, but always collectively. Relief washed over me as the mystery was solved, but then Mam said, "Do you hear her, Maeve? She's calling me."

When I looked perplexed by this statement, she said, "Your sister, Ishleen. It's her very self that will be coming to us again." She touched her belly with one hand.

"Nuala," my father said tenderly. "It isn't the same child."

"It is, Desmond!" Mam said with fervor. She gave him a look then as if his words were a betrayal. "I'm the one who bears the child in my body. I think I know better!"

Da looked stunned by the intensity in her voice.

There was the real world of the five senses, the factual world with all its borders and boundaries. Anyone of that real world who could hear it would say the voice was the murmuring of an isolated swan. But there was also the subtler world, which was also a world of the senses, but of infinitely more than five. And in that world, the voice was that of Ishleen, whom Mam was carrying for a second time; the sister who should not have died, and who ached to come back to us. I understood this all at once as the rain soaked me, and, looking into Mam's face, I could feel what she was feeling. Mixed with her anxiety was a vivid yearning, the desire I could feel so physically that it made my stomach seem to float in my body. As strong as it was, it was also elusive. And I remembered suddenly the day Mam and I had gazed out at the horizon and talked about this vague, unnameable yearning. What seemed strange to me now, and made no sense, was that it was the same feeling, as if it had always been Ishleen we'd been yearning for, even before the first Ishleen had been born.

Only Ishleen returning safe into this world would quell this desire in Mam. Only Ishleen could make the world be right again for her.

My father and brothers were under the awning, keeping dry while Mam and I stood out in the element, soaked and dripping. Turning and looking into my father's eyes, I felt my heart drop. All the certainty of what I'd just been feeling dissolved. Da's eyes were filled with fear and tinged with melancholy. I thought of the words I'd heard him speaking to Fingal the night before, that Mam's grief had affected her mind and she was not the same woman she had been a year ago.

I breathed deeply in the rain and was wrought with confusion, torn between the sense that I understood everything Mam felt, and the fear for her sanity. But I could hear the swan, and when I listened to it murmuring and humming, I wanted to believe that Mam was right, that it was whispering to her; that my sister, both dead and yet to be reborn, was speaking through it.

"Do you feel it, Maeve? How badly she wants to come back to us in this life?"

It frightened me how much I did feel it, and how intent and overcome Mam was with her certainty about the voice. I nodded, and knew my shivering was not caused by the rain.

CHAPTER 4

Mam and I had changed out of the wet garments. She had dried my hair and now she sat before the hearth staring into the fire, the pot of potatoes trembling on the boil, and I stood behind her drying her hair with a cloth.

Da had taken up repairing his net again, his big calloused hands working deftly, tying and knotting. Donal, who was helping him halfheartedly, suddenly looked up.

"I hear there are strangers in the village of Dunloe," he said, "and though they are not wearing uniforms, everyone is suspicious that they are English soldiers getting a good look around at the place."

"Da, we've got to be ready if they come to Ard Macha," Fingal said, and Da nodded in agreement.

They kept on their conjectures about the English

soldiers as if to distract themselves from their fears about Mam, but I saw their eyes flashing to and away from her.

Donal started talking about *The Book of Invasions*, about the successive takings of Ireland over the centuries.

"Why is Ireland always being invaded, Da?"

Da went still, his hands stopping their steady work. He looked up, his reddish hair glinting in the firelight like newly shined copper.

"She is wild, her land richer and greener than any other land, and her weather is moody." Da glanced at Mam. "She is superstitious and she is a fatalist. She cannot be fully conquered. The invaders know that, and it eats at them. Her soul is her own."

Mam was watching the steam rise from the boiling pot. A few droplets of rain still clung to her face and dripped from the ends of her long, dark hair. I had the sense that though Mam was pretending to be lost in her own thoughts, she was listening to every word Da said, and feeling all the meaning of it.

The potatoes were ready, and I helped Mam ladle them into bowls along with boiled fish. Instead of five places, Mam set six, placing an extra bowl of food between me and her.

"We'll leave the door ajar," she said, though the rain was still falling, "so she knows she's welcome."

Mam looked wistfully at the open door the entire meal, the threshold soaked, the earth floor around it going to mud. She raised her head high and strained to listen through the rain.

"I hear her again," she said.

My brothers set down their spoons very quietly, and a soft pall settled around us all. I could not bear to look at Da, knowing what I'd see in his eyes. Mam, sensing their discomfort, frowned, and a wrinkle formed between her eyebrows.

To change the subject, I said, "Did you see the little bottle I found in the ruins and gave to Mam?"

Mam fingered the bottle that hung around her neck, glowing softly.

The others looked at it. "There's something moving in it, like a flame," Da said.

"Yes." Mam grasped it possessively as Da reached across to touch it. "You know," she went on, not looking at Da but only at my brothers and me, "those ruins are not the remains of a convent as everyone says they are."

"I always imagined that it was a palace and a king ruled it," Fingal said.

"It *was* a palace," Mam said, "but you know as well as I do that it was a queen who ruled it, not a king."

"A queen?" Donal asked, raising his eyebrows and smiling, but unable to hide the indignant blush that had come upon his cheeks.

Even when my brothers were small, and Old Peig, the midwife who had brought us all into the world, first told us that a queen had once ruled Ireland, they'd scoffed at the story and insisted it was false. They still did not like the idea of women ruling Ireland.

"In the early times, women ruled Ireland, Donal, and the entire coastline was covered in primeval forest, trees everywhere, all the way down to the sand on the beach, flowers and fruit and fields of grain. When the trees were cut down, the queen went into exile. Now all one might harvest here is rock and shell. Even our little plots of potatoes and barley are won from difficult labor," Mam said.

"Old Peig!" Donal muttered, and rolled his eyes.

Fingal, the biggest skeptic of all, could not help but ask, "And that is because the queen fell, Mam?"

Fingal was not trying to sound condescending, but it was there always in his voice whenever Mam talked about things she called history and he called folklore.

I shouted out in defense of Mam. "A queen can rule and a queen can fall, just as a king can fall!"

"Maybe," Mam said, "with even more terrible consequences than when a king falls."

Da and my brothers went quiet again at the grave tone of Mam's voice.

"You've never heard in school of the great queens of Ireland? The first was the goddess Danu."

"Danu," Donal said. "Weren't she and her people defeated by the Milesians, who would rule the visible world, while Danu and her people, the Danaans, took possession of the invisible regions belowground and beyond the seas? Isn't it the old myth that they still rule those regions?"

"It's something like that," Mam said, "though I believe big important pieces are missing from the history books. The Holy Isles were established eventually, and Danu became remote from the people of Ireland, though she longs to return."

"But it's a myth, Nuala," Da said gently.

"How do you know that it's a myth?" Mam asked turning to him sharply. I could see by her clipped tone that she was very angry with Da.

"How could such things be real?" he asked.

Mam rolled her eyes. With my brothers she was a little more tolerant, but with Da right now, she was positively impatient. "There is more to the world than you can see directly before you, Desmond!" she cried, then pounded the table with her fist in exasperation.

There was a collective silence, which no one dared break.

Mam was very proud, and Da, I knew, had hurt her by dismissing her certainty that Ishleen would come to us a second time.

Donal shot Mam a pained look, and seeing it, Mam sighed, then said, in a softer tone, "But all that is hearsay. The ruins are what we were talking about in the first place. They were a convent, as we've always been told. A quiet hostel of nuns at prayer. After all, what good is a woman if she is not quiet?"

She gave Da a withering look, and his face fell. He hung his head.

I sat alone on my bed behind the curtain and carefully examined the triple-spiral stopper from the broken bottle meant for Mam. It was a single swirling unbroken line that formed three spirals, like the crest of one wave sitting on top of two others. I worried that the bottle meant for

me might not offer Mam all the protection she might need, so I put the triple-spiral stopper onto a string, then went out to her and told her I'd found it also at the ruins, and that I wanted her to have it.

Her eyes lit up, and she took in a breath, immediately drawn to it. Her hand shook slightly as she reached to take it.

"But don't you want it for yourself, Maeve?" she asked.

"No, Mam, it's for you."

I gazed at the bottle intended for me, glimmering around her neck, and yearned to have it again in my possession. But I could not ask her for it. She had been so moved when I'd given it to her. Besides, when I thought of the mysterious woman's concern for Mam, I knew Mam needed it more than I did.

Mam slipped out of the house in the middle of the night. I got up and saw my father standing at the open door looking down the cliff to the beach. It was the moonlight and the reflections of it on the water that illuminated Mam's figure, standing there on the black rocks looking out to sea, her forearms and hands pressed to her belly, the crystal bottle glowing softly between her breasts.

Very faintly from somewhere in the distance, I could hear the soft murmuring of the swan.

"Don't you hear it, Da?" I asked, and touched his shoulder.

He turned and faced me, his forehead fraught with distress. "Hear what, love?"

"The swan. Do you hear its voice?"

He gave me a piercing look, a further darkness cast over his brow.

"Not yourself as well, my girl," he said.

I felt a wave of panic move through me. "But I hear it, Da."

"You love your mother so much you think you hear something," he said. "But there's no sound other than the one we're always hearing: the waves breaking below on the shore."

That night, when Mam came back in, she did not sleep with Da behind the curtain in the box bed, but went into the byre and slept between the cow and her new black calf.

CHAPTER 5

he next morning, I stepped outside the threshold of our cottage to watch my father and brothers descend the cliff, making their way down to the sand and through the rushes, where they climbed into the small fishing boat and navigated the waters of the bay.

Close enough that the mists could not conceal it, a *skellig* rose from the sea, an isle of jagged peaks around which gannets and kittiwakes squealed and circled. When Ishleen was still alive, Old Peig had told us that long ago, the *skellig* was known as Woman's Crag.

"Sometimes," the old woman had said, "the goddess Danu herself came and stood there, looking longingly at Ard Macha."

Sailors and fishermen still reported apparitions there occasionally, of an otherworldly woman.

Today the birds around it screeched and called, rising in nervous clouds, circling and alighting again.

Often my father did not take the boat, but walked south on the headland to a shelf of limestone under an overhang of rocks, where he fished for black pollack. But this morning, in spite of the noise and riot of the birds around the *skellig,* the sea was still. I watched my brothers help him spread the fishing net.

I breathed in the soft air and sighed, then went inside, where Mam was sweeping the earthen floor.

Suddenly she stopped the broom.

"You know why the birds are screeching like that today, don't you, Maeve?" she asked.

When I looked at her, at a loss, she touched my cheek and said, "They hear your sister, too, through the voice of the swan."

With Mam's hand on my cheek, I could hear the very faint uttering of the swan, seeming to come from the air itself.

"We've got to do everything we can to help little Ishleen come safely back to us," she said. "We need to pick the herb that grows wild around the pagan stones."

Picking the vervain was looked down upon as a kind of pagan practice, but Mam did it anyway. She hated being dictated to, and, believing there was protective magic in it, she often dried and burned the herb.

"And we can leave a few offerings at the shrine of Saint Brigid, the patron saint of motherhood," I said to her, the shrine being near where the vervain grew.

Mam liked this idea, and we gathered a few things

together that we might use as offerings: seashells, small stones we'd collected on the shore over the years, buttons and stubs of candles. Mam reached for the comb decorated with rhinestones that Da had bought her in Killybegs before they'd married.

"You aren't going to part with that, Mam?" I asked. "Da gave it to you."

The color rose in her face, and she tightened her lips. "I don't like the way your da's looking at me lately, Maeve, like I've lost my senses, when the fact is, my senses have never been finer."

"Why don't you soften to him, Mam?" I pleaded quietly.

She hesitated, but still put the comb in the wicker basket. When Mam got proud over something, she was as unmovable as a mountain.

We left the cottage and walked the cliff road to the site of the shrine.

Mam lit a bit of candle and put it into a china cup to protect the flame from the wind, and left it before the weathered statue of Saint Brigid, who stood in a grotto of rock, long dry grasses trembling in the breeze around her.

"Maeve," Mam said. "Look, there's the new pastor, Father Cormac."

A thin, dark-haired figure was walking gingerly around the ancient stones, studying them earnestly, his hat pressed against his heart.

"How odd, Maeve. A priest in this place."

In church every week, our old pastor, Father Flanagan,

had discouraged anything at all that rang of old beliefs. From the road once, he had seen Mam here gathering vervain and had railed at her to keep away from the pagan stones on her way to the shrines.

After that day, Mam had stopped attending Mass. I think she got a secret pleasure out of bucking convention, and continued to wander freely among the stones, which some of the local women found scandalous. Da, and the rest of us, still went to Mass. Father Flanagan had died the previous winter and this new, young pastor had been sent to us.

Mam gazed at Father Cormac intently as he squatted down and touched one of the stones.

"He must be a good man, this new priest," she said softly.

It was then that Father Cormac turned and saw us there. Even at the distance we stood from him, I saw him blush to be caught here, but he rose up and smiled and waved his hat before he put it back on and walked toward us.

"You seem to understand something that our previous pastor did not, Father Cormac," Mam said.

"What could that be, Mrs. O'Tullagh?"

"That there's no great difference between the ancient saints and the new ones."

"Well, historically you are right, Mrs. O'Tullagh."

"Our Saint Brigid herself was originally the pagan Brigid, the goddess of mothers, smiths, poets and healers," Mam said with a ring of bravado in her voice.

"Yes, the world is a much more complicated place than many give it credit for being," he said, smiling widely at her.

"And you know also, Father, that a queen once ruled Ireland," she said.

"Yes, there were great queens once ruling here," he replied.

"Anyone else, Father, would deny that, would say that women were weak and dependent creatures."

"I'd never say that, Mrs. O'Tullagh," he said softly, and bowed.

I liked his pink face and mild blue eyes and his smile that made him press his lips together.

"Then you are a good and wise man, Father Cormac," Mam said. "So much so that I think I might like to go back to church next Sunday."

"I would be greatly honored if you did, Mrs. O'Tullagh," he said. "I hope to see you there."

He bowed to both of us and wandered down the road.

"Da would be thrilled if you went back to church, Mam," I said.

Mam stiffened at the mention of Da. "Your father thinks I'm mad."

"He doesn't, Mam."

"He does," she countered firmly.

I looked into the wicker basket and noticed we still had the comb.

"I'm glad you're keeping the comb, Mam," I said.

"I'm not keeping it. I'm just looking for a good place to

leave it. Not as an offering, just as something that needs to be let go of."

She wandered in among the pagan stones and threw the comb at a distance into the overgrowth. My heart sank, and I turned away. If Da didn't believe that Ishleen was coming back to us, how would he ever redeem himself in Mam's eyes?

"Maeve!" Mam cried out suddenly, pointing to something under what once must have been a druid altar. I ran to her. A swan was nested in a clump of moss and ferns, one injured wing lying across its side spread open like a fan.

"The poor creature's probably a victim of Tom Cavan's. He had a slingshot in his pocket when we found him yesterday," I said.

Mam knelt down before it, and it stood and stretched its full length and flapped its powerful wing, holding the other carefully extended. Swans when approached were usually cantankerous, but this one surrendered fully as Mam lifted it in her arms. It was of a placid, docile nature, unbirdlike in the way it looked at us, its eyes strangely human, watchful and aware.

Walking home along the promontory, we passed two townswomen, Mrs. Callahan and Mrs. Molloy, both of whom had been cold to Mam since she'd stopped attending Mass. They huddled next to each other when they saw Mam carrying the swan in her arms a few paces ahead of me, the creature uttering softly, and Mam, not caring an iota what the women thought, uttering back.

The two women began to whisper, and after Mam had passed them and I was about to, one of them said, "Nuala O'Tullagh's stone mad for sure."

The other replied, "And that daughter of hers is following directly in her shoes."

My heart plummeted. I tried to keep pace with Mam, but the words of the women kept repeating themselves, stunning me anew each time they did.

When we were near home, we saw Tom Cavan standing on the road watching us with his arms crossed. I stiffened, tightening my jaw as we passed him. I flashed my eyes in his direction.

"Are you responsible for this, Tom?" I asked.

He gave me that piercing, eerie smile. "Just for you," he said.

My face burned and I took a deep breath, but without the bottle near my skin, I could not seem to suppress my outrage. I felt the fury and frustration distorting my features. He snickered as we passed him.

Mam and I scaled the hill, and while she took the swan home, I stopped at the Cavans' cottage and knocked. Mr. Cavan opened the door. Farther into the room, Mrs. Cavan was stirring a pot over the fire.

"Tom did it again, Mr. Cavan," I said. "He never learns. He gets pleasure from injuring helpless creatures, and no one ever puts a stop to it!"

He looked at me gravely. "You're right, Maeve. There's a wharf man's job waiting for him in Ballyowen. It's time he grew up."

"No!" Mrs. Cavan protested.

"I'll not hear another word out of you about it, Eileen. He's going to Ballyowen in the morning."

I felt dazed as I walked home.

Mam carefully put the swan's wing into a splint, and we made a bed for it with rushes and soft blankets, and fed it oats. I lit a fire, and Mam and the swan settled near it, the swan resting its long neck over Mam's shoulder. It spoke in a quiet murmur, and Mam spoke back as if she understood.

"This creature reassures me greatly, Maeve," she said. "It is heavy and substantial, and its heart is big! You can feel it thudding."

I sat near her and admired the swan, touching its feathers, feeling the silken soft down when it shifted its wings, its bright amber eyes thoughtful and intelligent.

I was restless, alternately excited by the prospect of Tom's departure and haunted by the words of the two women.

When Da and my brothers came home, they were startled by the presence of the swan.

"This creature's just here to ensure that Ishleen arrives to us safely," Mam explained to them with a note of defiance in her voice. She'd not be dissuaded by their doubts. I longed to be as sure as she was.

I watched their eyes as they exchanged uneasy looks. Da settled before the hearth and stared mutely into the fire. I was afraid of this certainty he and my brothers seemed to feel about the unsoundness of Mam's mind, afraid of the powerful way that certainty held the air. If I breathed it enough, I wondered, would it persuade me, too? I did not want to face the spark of my own doubts.

Before dark, unable to bear it any longer, I escaped the oppressive air of the house and went out to the pagan stones. Mam was of an impulsive and fiery nature when she was angry. I knew that a time would come when she would regret throwing the comb into the field, so I searched for it in the overgrowth but could not locate it. Eventually I gave up and found myself drawn to the ruins. I wandered down there, around the tower to an archway with a broken wall, half crumbled away. There above, carved into the piece of lintel that remained, was a frieze of birds, mostly swans.

I wanted to get closer to it, so I carefully climbed what was left of a broken banister. Close up, the swans were carved, wings outstretched in permanent, graceful flight.

And then I heard something: a faint infusion of female voices, both there and not there. The harmonies produced were tremulous and high-pitched, and strangely familiar, though I could not recall where or when I had heard this chorus before.

I climbed down from the banister and stood absolutely still, listening very hard as the voices sounded and retreated, sometimes nothing more than an echo or a residue of sound, sometimes getting lost in the gusts and filling me with doubt that I had heard anything at all but the wind.

It was then that a slew of birds came flying in from Woman's Crag, screeching and honking. They flew over me where I stood, a riot of movement and sound, white feathers and floss floating down over me like snow.

Moments later, they departed, rising high up again on the air and crossing the sea, their forlorn voices fading into the distance.

Mam had said that the injured swan "reassured" her. This demonstration by the birds had flooded me with something I might also call "reassurance."

If Mam was mad, I thought, then I am mad, too, but now somehow I was not afraid. As I looked at the feathers all around me, I felt a sense of exaltation. I thought of the woman who had given me the little bottles, and how bits of pale gray down had drifted from her cloak.

CHAPTER 6

Over the coming months Mam carried the injured swan with her everywhere, even to church, and the same local women who had seen her and whispered about her stared. The appalled expressions on their faces were bad enough. But it was my father's and brothers' pained incomprehension that caused a rift in our house, and made Mam and me feel hopelessly distant from them.

I took over many of Mam's tasks: cooking, cleaning the ashes and sweeping the hearthstones, driving the cow and her little black calf to and from the field.

As her pregnancy advanced, Mam was uncomfortably hot and perspiring. Some nights she got up and opened the door, admitting the cold wind that came in and knocked things down, causing the empty kettle to swing on its crane and the hearth ashes to fly.

During her eighth month, an odd thing occurred. It was an unusually still night. I was fanning Mam, dabbing the sweat from her neck, when we heard hard, loud blows on the door. We awakened Da and my brothers, who had slept through the noise, but when they opened the door, nothing was there.

The next day, I returned home from driving the cows and found the swan in the cottage, but no sign of Mam. The necklace with the bottle had been left on the table. I grabbed it and, in a panic, ran outside.

Mam was standing knee-deep in the tide, her shoes on the foreshore as if they'd been flung there. She bent over and splashed her face in the frigid water.

"Mam!" I screamed into the wind, and she looked up.

Just as the tide was beginning to return seaward, I saw a shadow in the water. Mam stiffened as something grabbed hold of her and pulled her into the undertow. Falling into the rushing water, she struggled to get away.

I ran skidding down the hill, raising rocks and clods of earth. The new tide came in with force, throwing Mam back onto the shore, but as it retreated again, she was pulled so hard that this time she disappeared into the waves.

I ran in against the tide, falling to my knees, but making my way finally under, into the dark of the water. There was Mam, twisting and struggling, her hair and nightgown waving gracefully around her as she flailed.

Something had her by one ankle, and was drawing her into the dimness.

I saw a bloated but human-looking female face, ripples of greenish blond hair waving around it like an undersea plant. The rest of the monster, whatever it was, was hidden in the opaque shadow of the water. Suddenly it undulated from the waist, and I saw the flash of a huge fish tail.

Grabbing hold of Mam's other ankle, I thrust the bottle with its red, pulsating flame into the creature's face. Its eyes bulged and its nostrils flared as it let go of Mam, and it disappeared in a convulsion of bubbles, its frenetic shadow growing small far below.

I pulled Mam, still stunned and flailing, to the surface and, fighting the tide, brought her ashore. She was weak, drenched and breathing hard, pressing her palms against her swollen belly. With shaking hands I placed the necklace with the bottle on it around her neck.

As I led her up the hill, Mam told me to go and fetch Da from the rock cliffs to the south, where he was fishing for black pollack with my brothers. "Tell him to bring Old Peig to me."

Old Peig, a small, ancient figure leaning deeply on her blackthorn stick, sent my father and brothers from the house, saying that they were out of their element in the province of women.

Examining Mam, she concluded immediately that the baby was not yet ready to come.

I took orders from the old woman, arranging the

feather bed so that Mam was comfortable, putting the kettle on the fire and boiling a little porridge for the three of us.

The swan watched placidly as Peig sat at the foot of the box bed, dabbing an herbal concoction on Mam's feet and ankles where the monstrous creature had bitten her and sunk its nails.

"What creature was it?" the old woman asked.

"A woman, half fish," I said.

Peig's hands paused, and she looked into Mam's eyes.

"I told my husband, Peig, but he didn't believe me that the thing had a human face."

"Things have not been good between Mam and Da," I told Peig. "Mam's been sleeping in the byre."

Peig gasped with disapproval. "You'll stop sleeping in the byre immediately and take your place again in this box bed!"

Mam looked admonished and closed her eyes.

"Why do you keep the swan?" Peig asked Mam.

"It was injured and I brought it home to heal it. I've grown attached to it," Mam said. She shifted on the pallet, and the bottle around her neck caught the light.

The old woman pointed a wrinkled, trembling finger at it. "Where did you get this, Nuala?"

"Maeve found it at the ruins. I've been wearing it every day since."

"It's for protection," I said softly. "But she took it off today."

Peig looked thoughtfully at each of us. "Why did you take it off, Nuala?"

Mam shook her head. "I can hardly account for my actions, missus. I thought I'd burn up with the heat. I wanted nothing touching my skin. I almost lost all sense and tore the very gown from my body. I could think of no better refuge than the cold tide, then that awful creature grabbed me by the ankle."

Peig gave me a piercing look with her rheumy eyes.

"There's a shadow over Ard Macha," the old woman said gravely, "since the time when Ishleen died." She dabbed Mam's forehead with a cool cloth. "You mustn't get agitated, Nuala. You must get some rest. Maeve and I are here if you need anything."

When we heard Mam's steady breathing in sleep, Old Peig leaned toward me and whispered, "Tell me about the bottle. How did you come by it?"

"A mysterious woman gave it to me—a woman wearing white with feathers on her cloak. She gave me two bottles: one she said was for Mam, and the other, which Mam is wearing, was meant for me. She said they would protect us. When I was coming home, Tom Cavan surprised me and tried to take Mam's bottle. It fell and broke. Mam needed protection more than I did, so I gave her mine. On another cord around her neck, Mam wears the stopper from the bottle that was meant for her. It has a little symbol on it."

"Did you ask the woman why your Mam needed protection?" Old Peig asked.

I shook my head. "Looking back, there are many things I wish I had asked."

Old Peig got up and approached Mam's sleeping figure. Very gingerly she moved aside the fabric at Mam's chest until she was able to see the stopper. She came back quietly.

"It is an old Danaan symbol. Ard Macha has a mystical history that very few people know of, Maeve," she said. "And something very ancient has indeed resurfaced. The armor the men found in the bog, I believe, is an artifact of a terrible battle that was waged here seven centuries ago. But what I know about Ard Macha, though it is an incomplete history, begins long, long before that battle.

"In the beginning, Ireland was a place of primeval forests and oak groves. The original inhabitants were the Tuatha de Danaan, or the children of the goddess Danu. They were not mortals but another breed of human, a subtle people who worshipped trees and water, people who transformed themselves into birds to fly, or into seals or walruses to swim long distances across the seas.

"A less subtle people known as the Milesians invaded Ireland, battled Danu's children and drove the goddess and her people into exile. During the wars, many of the children of Danu who narrowly escaped the Milesians with their own lives fled Ireland in bird form or swam away in the water in the form of seals. Many went south by way of the Celtic Sea, settling in northwestern Spain, where, in their human forms, they intermarried among the Spaniards. Others flew far into the western seas, colonizing and establishing the legendary Holy Isles. But there was also an agreement made between Danu and the Milesians. Danu would keep a seat in Ireland. She chose as her sanctified place Ard Macha. She and her priestesses moved between the Holy Isles and her monastery here, which she came to every year at Samhain, just before the dark of winter.

"But another queen of mysterious origins came to try to defeat Danu and take her throne. There was a terrible battle. Neither was completely defeated, but each was injured enough by the other. That is all I know. But the residue of that evil queen remains here, just as the sacred residue of Danu is still with us in some distant ways.

"I don't know why the unearthing of that armor brought so much darkness to us, but it still contains power, and it's been unleashed upon the air." She was silent a moment, then asked, "What happened to that armor that was found?"

"It disappeared. Someone took it the very night it was unearthed. The men left it in the bog, and when they returned later, it was gone."

Old Peig stared a few moments into the dying fire, then looked again at the stopper. It began to glow, and she gazed at it, then closed her eyes and lifted her head, as if she were seeing something within her own mind. When she opened her eyes, she looked earnestly at me.

"You've got a lot of responsibility to shoulder," she said.

"What do you mean, missus? What did you see?"

"I believe it *will* be Ishleen coming back, just as your mam says. You'll have to be a very strong girl, Maeve. You'll have to be steadfast."

"Why, missus?" I asked.

But Old Peig just shook her head, then looked again at Mam. The Danaan symbol around her neck glowed in the firelight.

In spite of Old Peig's unsettling words, I slept deeply that night, but awakened when it was still dark. Mam and Old Peig were sitting up near the hearth, the embers of a fire still glowing.

"What is wrong between you and your husband, Nuala?" I heard the old woman ask.

"He thinks I'm mad, missus."

Peig peered at Mam, the firelight flashing on her face. "You need your husband now. You've got to forgive him."

"I can't, missus. It hurts me too much that he thinks I'm mad."

"It hurts your pride, Nuala, that is all."

"Isn't that enough?" Mam asked.

"No," Old Peig said plainly, and squeezed Mam's forearm with her gnarled, speckled old hand. "You love your husband deeply. Pride means nothing in the face of that."

But Mam looked unmoved. She averted her eyes from the old woman's.

"It's a weakness, Nuala, your pride. It's painful to those who love you," Peig said.

"It's painful to me that he doesn't believe me."

"Would you rather he lie to you? Desmond is skeptical of things that defy the five senses."

Mam held the old woman's eyes, and her face grew soft, until some thought seemed to overtake her. She sat up very straight and clenched her jaw.

Old Peig sighed and shook her head. "It's a weakness, Nuala."

The next night, Mam's pains were strong and steady, and it was clear that her lying-in time had come. Old Peig sent my father and brothers to sleep at the Cavans' cottage. With Tom no longer around, there would be room for them there.

Mam was about five hours in labor before the baby was born. As soon as the baby drew air and screamed, Peig showed her to me.

"It's her, Maeve. It's little Ishleen come back to us."

Peig placed her, wrapped in a blanket, in Mam's arms.

I stroked Mam's hair, my heart swelling with happiness. "Shall I fetch Da, Mam?"

When she hesitated, I looked at her anxiously, aching to see Da and Mam smile at each other and embrace.

"Right now I'd like to just lie quietly," Mam said.

"Oh, please, Mam!" I whispered.

"Oh, Maeve, there will be plenty of time for that in the morning."

"But, Mam, when he sees that it's Ishleen and apologizes, you'll forgive him, won't you?"

She looked at me in silence for a moment, then drew a deep breath and sighed. "Yes, I will, Maeve." Her eyes filled. She tensed her mouth, reached for my hand and squeezed it.

"All right, then," I said. "Mam, let me hold her awhile," I pleaded. "You sleep."

She handed me my tiny sister, then lay back and closed her eyes, but opened them again suddenly. "Wear these while you hold her." She took off the necklaces with the bottle and the spiral and gave them to me. Instead of putting them on, I placed them around Ishleen's neck. Mam fell asleep.

Old Peig lay down on the pallet spread for her near the hearth and dozed.

Ishleen twitched and cooed. She was so warm, and softer than the belly of a newborn calf. I studied her tiny, perfect features in the low light, her lips pursing like a little star. Her round, delicately veined head was bald beneath soft tufts of blond down.

Holding her securely in my arms, I laid my head back against the pillow and closed my eyes, inadvertently drifting off to sleep.

An intense chill came into the room. A strange woman was kneeling between me and Mam. I knew then that I was sleeping and struggled to awaken, but couldn't. At one point, the woman's dress brushed against my arm, and there was a slimy feeling to it, and a smell of the foreshore. Flapping its wings wildly, the swan began to cry out, but the woman overpowered it somehow, until it grew silent. No one awakened. The woman stared at Ishleen, and then at me. I suddenly saw her retreating between the curtains closed around us in the box bed.

I managed to open my eyes, but could not move. Ishleen was asleep, and so was Mam. The swan was gone. I could smell the odor the woman had brought in and could feel the chill she'd left behind her.

The rushlight dwindled low on the ledge, the flame about to cave into the hot wax. Most of the room was plunged into shadow.

With effort I was able to move. Very gingerly I got up and lit a fresh rushlight. That was when I noticed Mam's eyes, wide open and staring at nothing.

I shook her arm. "Mam! *Mam!*"

I pressed my ear to her heart and heard it beating very slowly and quietly.

I tried to awaken Peig, calling her name and shaking her arm, but she was heavy with sleep, her mouth open and drawing noisily at the air.

I ran to the Cavans' house and got Da. On our way back, we saw the swan lying dead on the rocky descent that led to the beach.

We were able to awaken Peig, but we could not awaken Mam.

CHAPTER 7

Mam was like a vacant shell. She stared through me into some remote distance. She could be slowly led places, and she would eat and drink when fed, but she had no will and seemingly no awareness of what was going on around her.

Da brought a doctor in from Killybegs, and when that one had no answers, he went as far as Galway to fetch another. That doctor was also at a loss.

I undertook to care for both Mam and Ishleen while my father and brothers fished or worked the ground, or cut turf.

I put the necklace with the triple spiral back around Mam's neck. I thought of returning the necklace with the bottle to her also, but feeling nervous for Ishleen, I wanted to protect her, too. Being so small, she wore the necklace awkwardly, so I wrapped it in soft wool and sewed it into a kind of sealed pocket on her nightgown, so it was always with her.

I was often whispering to Mam, touching her face, unwilling to believe that she could not hear or feel me there.

Mam, Ishleen and I slept together at night in the box bed. I sometimes startled from sleep, thinking I could hear Mam breathing at my ear. But usually it was the wind outside whistling between the stones, and sometimes it was a strong tide crashing at the rocks below. Or it was tiny Ishleen herself, drawing breath while she slept near me and mewing like a lamb. I held her to Mam's breast, where she nursed. When she finished, she fit easily into the curve of my arm and looked at me with shiny wet eyes, reflecting any embers still red in the hearth fire and the single candle lit nearby, a beacon, a tiny pulse of fire burning for Mam in hopes that she'd awaken.

One night, half-asleep, a kind of disembodied conversation took place, real or imagined, between myself and Mam. She wanted to know how Ishleen was.

"Are you here, Mam, in this room?" I asked.

"No. It is miraculous that you can hear me. I am far away from you."

"Where are you?"

"I don't know, Maeve. I can't see things clearly."

She told me that she was cold, that she didn't know

where she was or how she had gotten there, and that she could not stop shivering, though she seemed to be composed only of air.

A frigid breeze and two different smells accompanied her voice. The more mysterious one was like the fragrant dripping wax of burning candles, scented by some wood or flower. But mostly she brought with her the smell of pure cold. If ice or frost could have a smell, sharp, crystalline and intensely clean, it would be this fragrance Mam brought.

"It is very cold, but at least there's light. All around me most of the time there's light and there's movement. Wherever I am, I am not alone," she said.

"Who is with you?"

"No one I know, but they are all in the same condition as I am."

When I awakened, I wrapped Mam's body in blankets, but I feared this would do little to stop her disembodied self from suffering with the cold.

The next time one of these conversations took place, I was awake. I could hear Mam's spirit but could not see her. Was the sound of her voice on the air itself? Or was it somewhere inside me? I wondered. Where was she and why was she so cold?

Sometimes, when Ishleen would fuss or make little noises, the air around me got tense. I heard Mam take in her breath and sensed her listening.

During the day, I spoke to Mam, narrating to her little things that were happening.

"Mam, Ishleen is smiling," I'd say quietly, so that she might see this for herself if she was nearby.

It became habit, this speaking softly to Mam. My father and brothers exchanged looks when they heard me do it. I understood how Mam had felt when they'd thought she was mad.

One day while cooking at the hearth, Mam told me again how unbearably cold she was. "Try to see where you are, Mam, and I will come and get you," I cried.

I heard someone clear his throat. I turned and saw my brothers, having just come in, looking at me in horror.

"I'm not mad!" I barked at them, and they glanced away, but I knew when I turned around again that they would be exchanging looks. Still, I wasn't going to give up talking to Mam, and decided if they wanted to think I was mad, they could go ahead.

I couldn't stay angry with them for long. At least I could speak with Mam. The three of them had lost her completely and suffered over it.

During the day, I sometimes took Ishleen outside in my arms and peered down at the bay. Da and my brothers sat morosely in the boat, each lost darkly in his own thoughts. My father stared in a haunted way at Woman's Crag as gannets screeched and circled it.

At night before the hearth fire, Da rarely spoke and hardly ate or even tipped a glass of whiskey. I sometimes put Ishleen in his arms, thinking she'd give him some joy, and though he'd rock her gently for a few moments, he seemed at a loss and always asked me to take her back.

Fingal hardly acknowledged Ishleen. Now and then when she'd cry, he'd look across the shadows of the cottage at her in sullen bewilderment, then hang his head.

But it was Donal who brooded the most. The pain he felt made him anxious and combative. Donal knelt beside Mam trying, again and again, to awaken her. Once, as he was doing this, I saw lit threads between Donal and Mam igniting and fading and igniting again. When he got up and moved away from her, I saw the threads still attaching them.

"Donal is the softest of the three of you children," I was surprised to hear Mam's disembodied voice say to me.

"But he always seems so strong, so ready to fight," I whispered quietly.

"That's a way of hiding softness, Maeve."

One late afternoon after a day's work, Da and Fingal were somber when they came in. They sat before the fire, bearing their grief silently somewhere deep and hidden within.

"Where's Donal?" I asked.

"He's having a walk. He'll be home soon."

I looked outside and saw him throwing stones down the cliff toward the bay.

When he wasn't back by dark, I took a lamp outside and saw him swimming in the dangerous tides of the jagged shore, taking awful risks, tempting death.

I screamed for Da and Fingal, who went and yelled at

him over the noise of the swells until he came out of the water. When they brought him home, he was soaked by the tide.

"I wish an entire battalion of bloody English soldiers would come! I'd cut their throats by myself, every last one of them!" he said.

I gave him a cup of tea, and he dashed it against the hearthstones, shattering the crockery, the boiling water flying at me and burning my forearm.

I screamed, and my father yelled at Donal and shook him by the shoulders. "We are all hurt by what's happened, Donal. Not just you!"

There was a little butter on the shelf, and as tears of anger and grief fell from my eyes, I rubbed it into the burn. I knew Donal was already sorry. In my peripheral vision, I could see him looking at me. That was his way. He was fiery with impulse and angry with the world. But whenever his words or actions hurt me, he was always contrite. He never apologized out loud, but it was always in his eyes.

I stroked Mam's hair and she breathed quietly, her eyes always half open. It bothered me that Mam was left to lie most of the time in the box bed or sit in a chair with her head bending forward. I hated leaving her alone when I went outside.

She could be led places walking, but it took so much time because she moved so slowly and only when urged.

One night as we had our tea, I said to Da and my brothers, "We've got to make a special chair for Mam, a chair with wheels." They all gawked at me. "I want to be able to take her outside and down to the beach. I don't want to leave her here alone if I have to go far."

My idea was met with silence. Undaunted, I drew a picture of the chair I imagined. "She should go out for air and be near the tides. She should come with Ishleen and me when we pick mussels from the stones."

"What's the point of it? She isn't aware of anything around her," Donal said.

"How do you know that?" I asked angrily. He stared, wide-eyed, at me, then hung his head and seemed ashamed.

In spite of my irritation with him, I kept talking, but was met with more silence.

To try to create a dialogue about the chair, I pointed to Mam's old rocking chair and said, "This would be perfect if we could have wheels put on it."

Immediately both brothers objected with technical reasons why that was a ridiculous suggestion.

"Something like a wheelbarrow might work," Fingal said.

"A *wheelbarrow*? I'll not have Mam lying in a wheelbarrow. She needs a chair."

"Maybe another kind of chair, not a rocker, could have wheels put on it," Donal said. "Invalids have iron chairs."

"Yes, something like that. What do you think, Da?" I

asked, but he remained silent, drinking his tea and staring into the fire.

But that night as I was getting ready for bed, he called me over to him.

"We'll go to the blacksmith on Saturday to ask about a chair with wheels."

I threw my arms gratefully around him. As I was about to go, he said my name. I stopped and looked at him, but he kept his eyes on the flames in the hearth.

"Do you think she forgives me?"

"Oh, Da," I said. "I know she does. She told me so that very night after Ishleen was born." He stared at the flames with damp eyes, not seeing them.

That Saturday, Old Peig came to keep her eye on Mam, and the rest of us went by pony and trap to Killybegs.

When we got out of the trap and were walking to the blacksmith's up a street adjacent to the wharf, Da pointed out a little shop with lace curtains in the windows: Muldoon's Fine Imports. It was an anomaly among the other rough buildings, as if it had been lifted from some cultured place.

"That's where I bought a gift for your mam once," he said.

"A comb?" I asked. "With little jewels on it?"

His eyes widened. To hear it described seemed to stir him. "Yes," he said. "Do you know what ever happened to the comb?"

"It's at home, Da," I said. "You know how much Mam loves it."

He stared at the glimmering windows of Muldoon's and went very far away in his thoughts.

I remembered Mam describing this shop to me. I could see, through an open curtain, a shelf lined with colorful bottles and trinkets.

"They have scent in heart-shaped bottles," Mam had told me. "Imported from across the Irish Sea."

"Can I look inside, Da?" I asked.

He nodded, and while he and my brothers loitered outside the door, I went in holding Ishleen in my arms, never thinking to give her to Da to hold, so much had she become an extension of me. My arms had grown used to being sore from carrying her.

I hardly breathed at the sparkling atmosphere of the shop, little blue and crimson bottles and jars, oval-shaped soaps in porcelain dishes, the air smelling of dried roses.

I turned at the end of an aisle and found myself in the doorway of an attached room, a seamstress's shop where a woman was engaged in sewing hems. She looked up and nodded at me invitingly, and I stepped in, browsing through bolts of fabric. I stopped suddenly. On a headless dummy between two curtains stood an extraordinary dress, fashioned of what looked like bronze velvet and strips of gold and deep crimson silk. It was stately beyond any garment I had ever seen. Around the waist hung a belt heavy with metallic embellishments.

From an oblique angle, I moved in closer to it. "What's it made of?" I asked breathlessly.

"It's made of metal, but very finely wrought, so it looks like cloth unless you get close."

I had seen drawings of such dresses, but not nearly as beautiful, in the book that Donal had about medieval heroes.

As if reading my thoughts, the woman said, "Such a dress is for a woman on an adventure, don't you think? A woman who has an urgent quest."

She stood up, then led me to a spot about one foot directly behind the dress. Taking sleeping Ishleen from my arms, she told me to look straight ahead. In front of the dress was a mirror in which I could see my head and neck reflected. If I looked fleetingly, I could experience the impression that I was seeing myself wearing the dress. My image hit me like a bolt of lightning; my heart pounded with a mysterious feeling of expectation. For a reason that I did not understand, associating myself with the dress filled me with a surge of possibility. The dress exuded the temperature and aroma of cold: sharp and crystalline, as if it had been in the same place where Mam was captive. It was, as the seamstress had suggested, the dress of a strong, adventurous woman. In such a dress I might travel to unknown frozen regions and rescue Mam.

Someone else had come into the room, but I disregarded whoever it was and reached out to touch the fine metal of the dress with curiosity and fervor. A familiar womanly voice came from the new presence in the room. "Maeve."

Turning with a gasp, I saw Mrs. Cavan looking at me with raised eyebrows and a half smile.

"What an extraordinary dress," she said.

The seamstress, still holding Ishleen, looked perturbed by Mrs. Cavan's presence. The smile had fallen from her face. She carefully handed Ishleen back to me.

"It must cost dearly," Mrs. Cavan added, gazing at the dress with intense interest. Her eyes flashed in my direction.

"Maeve!" Da called, leaning his head into the shop. "Let's be getting on."

As I moved toward the door, I caught my true reflection—my rough rust-colored flannel skirts, my old boots covered in mud—and my heart fell slightly.

"Maeve," Mrs. Cavan said, stopping me. "I received a letter from Tom. He asked me to send you his regards."

I nodded, and in a barely audible voice thanked her, trying to continue on my way. But she stopped me again.

"Shall I send him your regards?"

I paused, but could not make myself agree to this. "No. Please don't," I said, and rushed to meet Da at the door.

The blacksmith's shop, bare-walled and smelling strongly of leather, shocked me back into the real world. In a daze, I showed the blacksmith my drawing. He nodded, then he and Da got into a conversation about the complications of making such a chair, and the price. I noticed Donal and Fingal looking through a half open door near the back of the shop, where I could hear a man speaking in covert but fiery tones. I went and stood with them, looking in. The orator had long hair and curly sideburns, and wore a wool cap with a brim set over his forehead. He sat on a stool addressing a group of seven or eight other men.

"Queen Elizabeth the murderess, daughter to the devil himself, Henry the Eighth, has new plans for invading Ireland. Living here as you do on the rocky western edge of our land, you haven't yet seen too many of the English soldiers. But news of their approach is always on the air, and getting stronger. They're determined to establish English control, limiting all forms of Irish independence."

"The devils," a few men muttered.

I followed my brothers as they stepped into the room, giving grave and respectful nods, extending their hands and introducing themselves.

"Emmet Leahy," replied the man who got up from the stool and stood before us like a tower. Though there were certainly tall men in Donegal, this one had to be half a head taller than the tallest.

When we sat, Emmet Leahy continued to speak. "The rebellion has ended in the south with the murder of the earl. Clanawley is now a wasted land."

"I'd like to join the mercenary army!" said Donal.

"So would I," Fingal said.

Emmet Leahy smiled at them. "I admire your spirits, young men, but there is something we need more of in this area right now. We must be organized. We need a faction, a steady meeting where news can be shared and plans made."

"We will be in charge of that," Donal volunteered.

Da appeared, and my brothers introduced him to Emmet Leahy.

I sat in the corner, rocking Ishleen, and the conversation continued about how the faction might work. That was when I had the vision for the first time. I saw myself in the dress, walking through an elegant interior blasting with drafts of cold wind, calling out to Mam, who called back to me from some vague distance.

Now and then I'd blink my eyes and focus on the real world. Da, my brothers and Emmet Leahy leaned forward in their chairs, facing one another. Donal was the one stoking the flames of the long conversation with his endless questions.

Indulging the dream a second time, I saw the seamstress from Muldoon's. In the vision she had delicate white feathers at her temples growing directly from her hairline, just as the woman who had given me the bottles had. As I was imagining this, Ishleen stirred. I lifted her up so she could look around the room, and a bit of soft white down floated from her blanket and drifted on the air around us before dropping slowly to the floor.

From that hour, Donal and Fingal stopped their brooding and their harsh tempers. Everything that had ever engaged their hearts and imaginations about Irish rebellion was suddenly given specificity and immediacy. Here was an opportunity to forge a path, and they threw every bit of themselves into it with great energy and seriousness.

Before we left Killybegs, I asked Da if we could stop again at Muldoon's Fine Imports. My heart raced as we approached the quaint facade with the tiny lights twinkling within. But I found the door locked fast. I knocked hard again and again, but no one answered.

Da smiled at me and said, "You must really like looking at those dainty things, Maeve."

"Yes, Da," I said, staring through the dim windows.

"We'll come back again sometime," he said.

Confused by my reluctance to leave, my brothers looked ponderously at me. I wanted to tell them, but I knew they'd think I was madder than ever. I missed Mam intensely.

When we were well on the road back to Ard Macha, and my brothers were talking excitedly to Da about Emmet Leahy, I whispered, "Mam, I'm going to find you. I'm going to bring you back to us somehow. You must be so tired of shivering with cold."

I could not get the dress out of my thoughts. Two days later, I took Da aside and told him about it. "I'm sure it costs dearly. I don't know how much, but the woman there was very kind, and perhaps she could work out some special arrangement with us. Could you just come with me, Da, to look at it?"

I knew better than to tell him I had imagined myself rescuing Mam from the cold place where she was prisoner.

"All right, love," he said. "We'll go and have a look."

The following week, Da took me back to Killybegs. Muldoon's Fine Imports had closed down. Every glimmering curiosity, every scrap of thread, was gone.

CHAPTER 8

shleen grew into a little enigma: a fairy of a creature with a head of wild wheat-colored curls, shot here
and there with red. She crawled early and walked early,
driven by curiosity and an impatience to be engaged in
the world.

When Ishleen was four and I was nineteen, she was
fascinated by fire and the sparking of the embers. With
great concentration and an awed silence, she watched the
black-encrusted kettle above the flames come to a trembling boil.

Being small, she did not really understand what was
wrong with Mam and spoke to her just as I did, combing
her fingers through Mam's hair. When we sat out near
the beach, she decorated Mam with tiny seashells and
sometimes with gorse flowers or maidenhair ferns.

Not only did Ishleen speak gently to Mam's inert body, but she addressed the air itself when we were far from Mam, in the same way I did, thinking Mam might hear.

Ever since I had seen the dress in Killybegs, I drew pictures of it with a piece of sharpened charcoal. Paper was scarce, so I used the blank back or front pages of the books Donal hoarded near his bed. But when there were no more blank pages in those, I took to drawing the dress again and again over the written text, and this Donal refused to tolerate.

One bright windy morning, while pushing Mam's wheeled chair out near the ruins, I discovered a wall of smooth flagstone that set my heart racing. I took out the charcoal that I kept with me always and began to sketch a life-size version of the dress on the wall before me. I gave Ishleen a piece of charcoal, too, and she set to scribbling with it on the wall near the ground. Seeing the life-size drawing of the dress filled me with euphoria and expectation.

"Mam," I whispered, and turned the wheeled chair so that she faced the dress. "I've seen myself wearing this dress and rescuing you."

I visited the drawing every day and added to it. If the rain partially erased the drawing, I drew it again. Since it had not fully faded each time, it began to take on many layers, growing more and more dimensional.

Though it thrilled me to see the drawing become vivid,

it frustrated me as well. It seemed so real, but it wasn't there at all.

And even worse than that, Mam had gradually begun to speak to me less often and was quieter when she did, as if her energy were fading. And to my horror, along with the smells of guttering candles and ice, an unpleasant odor sometimes accompanied her, something vaguely rancid.

I would speak obsessively to the air, hoping for an answer from Mam, while serving the dinner or stoking the embers. My brothers had grown so used to it that they'd taken to calling me "Mad Maeve."

At first Da barked at them for it, but over time, he stopped.

None of them understood what was happening to me, and I didn't, either. I only knew that I couldn't bear the idea of losing Mam.

It was just at this time that Tom Cavan, who'd been gone several years, was seen near dawn one morning in Ard Macha, carrying a spade and a lamp, his body and clothes covered in damp peat. That day I heard that the bog where the local men cut turf had been desecrated, and that the sky had been thick with vultures circling overhead. I went down there with Da and my brothers to look. Rough clods had been dug up and carelessly piled and scattered.

"He was clearly in search of something," Da said.

"Some other ungodly relic, most likely," Donal said, "but for what purpose, it is impossible to know."

The closer I got to the bog, the more distinctly I could smell rot on the air. It was the same smell that had been there when Tom had unearthed the armor years before. I was stunned when I realized that it was similar to the rancid odor I had gotten a vague whiff of recently, when Mam's presence had come.

"He found something," I said suddenly.

"How do you know?" Da asked.

"I recognize the odor."

Da and my brothers banded together with the local men and knocked on the Cavan door that day, but Mrs. Cavan said, "If he came to Ard Macha, he's left again, for I haven't seen a hair on his head."

As they were leaving, Mrs. Cavan called out after them, "If you see him, send him directly to me. I miss him something desperate." She made the sign of the cross.

No one saw him after that. As far as anyone knew, he was gone again.

Something was going on, I was certain. It was the rancid odor that terrified me for Mam, and I decided that I had to do something. I had tried to figure out where Mam's self, or spirit or soul, was but had not been able to. The one thing I had in my power to do was to get a dress or make one, as similar to the dress in my vision as possible.

I pleaded with Da to take me to Killybegs, to any shop at all where I might buy sewing supplies, hoping to find the delicate metal fabric that had formed the dress at Muldoon's.

"It's about bringing Mam back," I said.

"How, Maeve?"

"I saw it in my mind," I said. "I was wearing a dress like the one I saw that time, and I was rescuing Mam."

He looked at me with an expression of surrender. "I worry about you, Maeve, as I once worried about your mam. But in the end, she was right about Ishleen. I'm going to trust this desperate feeling in you."

Da took me to a shop in Killybegs, but there was no metal fabric like it, and the people we asked said they'd never heard of such a thing.

I had to settle, in the end, for a strong silk with metallic sheen.

It cost Da dearly.

Though I had little skill at sewing, for two days and two sleepless nights, I struggled my best, cobbling together a dress as similar to the one at Muldoon's as I could.

I finished it in the middle of the night when everyone was asleep. It fit me like a poor replica of the original. Still, I wore it outside. Carrying a lamp, I wandered the ruins and the surrounding shore where I'd once seen the mysterious woman who had given me the bottles.

For six hours or more, I went to every place I could imagine the woman might come, but nothing happened. I found myself growing more and more despondent over the hours, all my certainty draining away. I felt lost, my task hopeless.

As I went back in the direction of the hill, it began to rain. Just as dawn was breaking, I saw my father and brothers come out dressed for the downpour in their hooded oilcloth coats, getting ready to fish. I was soaked in my homemade dress.

They stood still when they saw me in my despondency. Somehow they seemed even more appalled than usual.

I swept past them and went inside, where I found Ishleen awake.

"Mam," I pleaded to the inert, wistful figure whose eyes looked hopelessly past me into some unknown vision. "What do I do?"

The hope that had gripped me now for so long regarding the dress was utterly gone, and I wondered about my own sanity.

I sat down before the fire, shivering in the soaked dress, and cried. Ishleen touched my shoulder. When I did not stop crying, she went and opened the door. Miraculously, the sun had come out and was lighting the world, a clear day in high summer. I got up and looked out. The sea where my father and brothers were casting their net was as calm as new milk.

I took the dress off and hung it outside on the line to dry in the clement air. As it stirred there on a faint breeze, the poorly crafted garment looked sad and deflated, the bodice caved in, the shoulders and arms slumping unevenly. Silk, I realized, should not get wet like that. The sheen was gone, the cloth pocked and wrinkled. What had I thought I could create? And even if I had created something close to the majestic dress at Muldoon's, what, then, would that have meant? I felt as though I had fallen from a great height.

I went back in and lay down in the box bed, leaving my chores and responsibilities on hold, and fell into a heavy sleep.

Later in the day when I awakened, the dress had gone missing from the line. I did not go in search of it, and in some perverse way was relieved by its disappearance.

"Probably the wind has blown it away," I said to Ishleen, though it had been a still day with only mild breezes.

A week later, Tom Cavan's mother, short and bent and wearing a flowered scarf on her head, came to our door.

"I'm taking a pony and trap into Dungarven tomorrow, Maeve, to buy fabric to make new curtains. Wouldn't you like to be coming along?"

I was surprised by the kindness of the gesture. Mrs. Cavan had never offered to help me with Mam or Ishleen. I knew she had always resented me for having told her husband about Tom's transgressions, and I knew she felt I was responsible for his having been sent away from Ard Macha. But maybe, having heard that my spirits were low, she'd softened to me.

"Thank you, Mrs. Cavan," I said. "I would like to come."

When I told Da about it later, he said, "I've a few

emergency coins stashed away. Why don't you take them and buy yourself some small trinket?"

I hugged him. He'd been worried about how sad I'd been lately.

The shop in Dungarven reminded me of Muldoon's Fine Imports. Both were situated on rough-and-tumble wharves, where rope, tackle, leather and farm supplies were sold. The shop was, as Muldoon's had been, an anomaly encased in its own mist.

A bell rang when we opened the door. The shop matron looked up at us in acknowledgment, but was busy speaking to two other customers dressed in lavish clothes, a mother and a daughter.

Mrs. Cavan went directly to some little glass bottles while I veered away toward a mirror, which I approached nervously. We had no mirrors at Ard Macha; in the past few years I had seen only the faint smear of my reflection at home in the copper pot, so it was always distorted. The self looking out from the other side was different from the reflection I'd seen years before at Muldoon's. My cheekbones were more prominent, my features were no longer soft but defined, and all over my nose and cheeks there was a light dusting of small freckles. There was something grave about my expression.

Gradually, the longer I looked, the less I thought of the reflection as being me. This image, I thought, gave the impression of someone formidable and complicated. I felt envious of this other in the mirror, as if she lived in the atmosphere of glimmering lights, an entirely different, more powerful and elevated existence than the one I lived. And as I stared at her, she wore the metallic dress and was standing in a vast frozen room. I heard a chandelier tinkling in the cold around her. The vision dissolved suddenly, leaving me in confusion.

I left the mirror and approached the bottles of scent, watching with absorption as the mother and daughter, wearing an elaborate system of scarves and jackets, huddled and gasped over the various perfumes, applying them to their wrists and squealing as they smelled them. The intense, almost cloying scent of flowers distressed me. The hems of their skirts were embellished with frills of lace, and I wondered why they would expose such fine lace to the certainty of mud. How did they manage to remain protected from it? That such a thought would occupy my mind made me think of how out of place I was here.

I moved off and looked at creamy ovals of soap displayed in a cut crystal bowl. With a tentative and trembling hand, I stroked the rounded surface of one of the soaps.

Suddenly Mrs. Cavan was at my side. She peered closely into my face and squeezed my wrist.

"I have a confession to make, Maeve," she said. "I didn't really come here for fabric. I've come for only one reason. I'd like to buy you something."

I gazed at her, hardly believing my ears.

"You're so lovely a young lady, and I think you deserve to have something nice. You see, Tom is coming home."

For a moment I did not understand the connection.

"Why is he coming back, Mrs. Cavan?" I asked. "He doesn't like to fish or work the ground." She remained quiet, looking at me. I suddenly understood what was happening, and my heart dropped.

"Tom has done well for himself. He sent me the money to buy you any gift you like. Even if it's a dress, I'm happy to purchase it for you. He says it was you who inspired his success. He no longer needs to fish or work the ground. He has wealth, and you know he's had his eye on you since you were children. You are nineteen and he is twenty-one, both good ages to marry. So," she said, "pick out a gift."

"You're too generous, Mrs. Cavan, and as much as I'd like to, I can't accept." I gave her an unwavering look.

Her eyes flashed, and I knew she registered my reluctance in regard to her son.

"There are other local girls who would be thrilled—"

"I know there are," I said plainly, unmoved. "Maybe he should ask one of them."

She took a deep breath and seemed to decide not to let this dissuade her. "I saw you looking at this," she said, pointing to the oval of cream-colored soap I had touched. "You'll at least let me buy this for you."

She asked the shop woman for a single cake of it, and I watched as it was wrapped in tissue paper and placed in a pale lavender box embellished in gold ribbon.

"I'll pay for it," I said, and pulled out the coins from my pocket, placing them on the counter. The shop woman looked at them, then narrowed her eyes at me. The corners of her mouth strained.

"It's fourpence ha'penny for this soap," she said, giving me a condescending look. "This soap is *French!*"

Mrs. Cavan laid a shilling on top of the coins, and the hard look melted from the woman's face.

As we traveled back to Ard Macha in the pony and trap, I thought of the silliness of the pampered girl and her mother, the meanness of the shop matron. The atmosphere had lost its heightened sparkle for me. And worst of all, the beautiful soap in its exquisite package had lost its sensual incandescence and had become nothing more than a fragrant-smelling bribe. Mrs. Cavan saw me as the wife of her mean-spirited son. Rarely had she shown me any kindness before. Why had I imagined there had been some pure intention behind her offer to take me to Dungarven?

All the way home, though, she made attempts to engage me in chatter. I sat leaning to one side, staring at the passing fields.

It was dusk when we arrived back at Ard Macha. I thanked Mrs. Cavan and was about to scale the hill when I was startled to see Ishleen talking to a woman in a gray-green dress down near the beach.

"Who is that woman?" I asked.

Mrs. Cavan stared darkly, and I felt that she knew who the woman was but wouldn't say. Her expression made me afraid for Ishleen, and I began running toward the beach.

"Ishleen!" I cried, but she was too near the roaring tides to hear me.

The woman spotted me coming and grabbed Ishleen's arm. In that moment there was a sudden commotion of birds—swans and falcons and herons flying overhead, feathers and down from their wings floating and descending around Ishleen and the woman. As birds alighted at various places on the stones, a swan landed at the feet of the woman in gray-green. It thrust out its chest and beat its huge wings, and as it did, it transformed into the woman who had once given me the little bottles. The woman in gray-green let go of Ishleen's hand and backed away several steps, then dove into the sea.

As I ran toward them, the birds that had alighted rose again into the air, and the woman in white turned back into a swan, rising with the others and flying in arcs over the sea as I took Ishleen into my arms. From that moment on, I would think of the woman who had given me the bottles as the Swan Woman. We watched her and the others flying into the distance, the evening sky gone almost fully dark.

Ishleen said she did not know who the woman in gray-green was, but that she had promised to take Ishleen to the place where she said Mam's soul was waiting for her.

The next day when I was driving the cows back up the hill, Tom Cavan jumped out from behind the wall, startling me so badly that I screamed. After I caught my breath, I was amazed by the way he was dressed: in an elegant, long fitted coat with tails, crafted of sky-blue velvet. His light brown hair was longer and carefully combed, the curls keeping their shape stiffly in spite of the wind. Though still recognizable as the boy who had taunted me all my life, he was now a man and he looked different, much taller and wider in the shoulders. The bone structure of his face was stronger, and he wore a mustache on his upper lip.

"Aren't you glad to see me back, Maeve? My mother told me what a beauty you've become, and she was right." He took a step in my direction.

"Stay away from me, Tom Cavan!" I cried, all my frustration and fury directing itself at him.

"You have spirit, and I've always liked that!"

"Stay away from me!" I practically spit the words at him, and now his face darkened.

"You'd like to leave here, wouldn't you? You'd like doctors for your mam, and nice things for your sister and yourself."

"Why are you dressed like that?" I was about to tell him that he looked like a right idiot, when I suddenly felt afraid of him. Maybe it was the faint wafting of the unpleasant odor, apparent now and again from behind the strong cologne he wore, that made me think he was responsible somehow for what had happened to Mam. It seemed to me that he and his mother were involved in some way with the woman who'd tried to lure Ishleen toward the sea.

I rushed away from him, suddenly terrified to have left Ishleen alone.

CHAPTER 9

I told my brothers and Da that Tom Cavan was bothering me, and that I was afraid he might try some mischief with me if I was left on my own caring for Mam and Ishleen. That got them riled up and angry, and after that, Donal and Fingal alternated days staying home.

Tom sometimes watched from a distance as Donal or Fingal walked the cows with us, cut peat or dug and planted.

We enjoyed this privilege for three days, and then at dusk on the third evening, while both brothers were down at the beach helping Da haul in his catch, I heard the cow mooing anxiously from the byre. I went and checked and saw that her calf had broken through a loose board and gone off on its own.

I went outside and, raking the distances with my eyes,

spotted the calf far off in the valley. A certain sweet flower grew down there in profusion around the dolmen stones near the vervain, and this little devil of a calf had a terrible sweet tooth.

The clouds were edged in red from the lowering sun, and there was still enough light in the sky for me to go without a lamp. I grabbed a rope and ran down after her.

Knee-deep in the flowers, her jaw working hard as she chewed, the calf blinked and gave me an irritated look, then twitched against the rope as I tried to secure it around her neck. She slipped loose and ran, tripping me so I fell into the flowers. I watched her prance up the hill, hopping more like a goat than a calf, in the direction of her mother's bawling moo.

As I stood up, brushing myself off, I heard a man's low groan. I froze and, listening expectantly, heard it again.

"Help me," the man said weakly.

About a yard away from me, just beyond a group of standing stones, rose an embankment of earth. I had always thought that the hole past that mud wall may have been bog land in centuries long past.

I looked down into the dim hollow and saw a man lying on his side, blood on his shirt and vest. He lifted his head, turning it slightly to look at me. With a shock, I recognized him as Denis Hayes, a member of the neighboring faction of the secret rebellion. He had come once to a meeting at our cottage.

"Mr. Hayes!" I whispered.

"The English . . . invaded us in Dunloe, tied us up.

Took food and supplies. I fought one of them and he shot me. . . ." He winced, tensing his entire body with suffering. He was about to speak again when I stopped him.

"I'm getting my da and my brothers," I began, but before the words were completely out of my mouth, we heard the pounding gallop of approaching horses.

"Hide!" he said. "For the love of God, hide, and don't show yourself for the world! They'll kill you as soon as look at you!"

I got on my knees, quickly creeping in the tall grass past the embankment and then behind a large standing stone.

The galloping came to a sudden halt, and I heard voices as the men dismounted.

One voice got closer to me, and I went as hard and still as the stone I leaned against. A shadow loomed on the ground, and the approaching Englishman's breathing grew audible. My muscles burned and ached with tension. I saw the contours of his boot, so close was he to me.

"Roberts! Come over here," the more distant voice called. "Look what I've found."

The shadow was gone suddenly, and a ruckus broke out. I heard them beating Mr. Hayes, dealing him kicks and blows. My impulse was to jump up and scream at them, but I knew they'd kill me. If he could just survive, I kept thinking, I'll nurse him back to life! I squeezed my eyes shut and covered my ears.

"Stinking Irish pig!" one of the Englishmen said.

I clenched my jaw to keep myself from yelling.

Everything stopped suddenly. I heard them mount horses and gallop away.

I got up and ran like mad, gesturing wildly at my father and brothers just as they were climbing the hill back home.

When they did not return right away with Mr. Hayes, I filled a skin with water, wrapped bread in a cloth and made my way back down. The daylight was almost gone. Moving in the direction of the lamps, I ran into Donal. I could see by the somberness of his demeanor that Mr. Hayes must have died.

"I'm coming up to arrange for a pony and trap. We're taking his body back to Dunloe."

Emmet Leahy arrived the next day. Donal, Fingal and Da and the other five men who'd been meeting for the past four years gathered in our cottage.

I knelt beside Mam, who sat unmoving in her chair, her head leaning to one side, and explained to her who was there and the importance of the meeting that was about to take place.

"It was awful, Mam," I said softly, "the way the poor man suffered."

"Does she understand what's being said?" one of the men who'd been watching me with Mam asked Fingal.

"I don't think so," Fingal remarked, shooting me an irritated look.

"She does!" I snapped. "She understands!"

Ishleen sat at Mam's feet, drawing with charcoal on a flagstone. Now and again, she'd get up and hold her drawing before Mam's face. "Look, Mam, I've drawn flowers for poor Mr. Hayes."

"The situation is dire," Emmet Leahy was saying to the men. "Hundreds of Irish have died of starvation in the south because of all the English raids and disturbances. Now they're up here in the north committing their dirty deeds."

Fingal, listening thoughtfully, sat at the hearth raking the cinders, then stirred the torpid coals until they glowed, the fire reviving.

The door was suddenly pushed open from the outside, and Tom Cavan appeared. He wasn't dressed in the odd, over-elegant manner he'd been in lately, but in the rough woolens and cap of an Ard Macha fisherman.

"This is an open meeting," Emmet Leahy said. "You are welcome."

Donal stood, ready to protest, and exchanged glances with Tom's father, who was in attendance.

Tom gave his father and Donal a gloating look, then sat negligently in a chair.

"The Spanish are our allies against the English," Emmet Leahy went on. "There is an ancient and powerful tie between the Spanish and the Irish. The northwestern coast of Spain has the same roots as we do in a Celtic mysticism, and we share with them a justified hatred for the English. If two very different countries can be soul mates, it is Ireland and Spain."

Tom Cavan listened to this information with absorption.

Emmet Leahy continued, "We've received calivers and gunpowder from Spain, and also from Scotland. We've no choice but to arm the people rather than rely solely on mercenary soldiers. And after we've distributed the guns to each cottage in the area, I'm off with plans to infiltrate an English fort in Skibbereen. I'll need to be asking for a few volunteers to go with me."

Donal and Fingal immediately raised their hands, and Leahy gave a nod of assent.

"We should talk about our strategy," Emmet Leahy said.

Donal looked at Mr. Cavan, who stood, then approached Leahy and took him aside, conferring for a few moments. Leahy then approached Tom. "I've met with all these men before. I'll be glad to come around and speak with you privately afterward. But for now, the rest of this particular meeting is closed."

Glaring at his father and then at Donal, Tom said, "Such important men you are. What would any secret rebellion do without the likes of two such as yourselves?"

Everyone in the room looked warily at Tom, especially his own father, the color high on his face.

"You especially will be sorry," Tom said, pointing angrily to his father. "I'll find some way of making you suffer."

He went out the door, slamming it after him.

"Can we expect worse from him?" Emmet Leahy asked Mr. Cavan.

"I don't think there's treachery in him," Mr. Cavan answered. "But he's up to something, and he is a mystery to me. He leads an entire life that I don't know about."

Emmet Leahy patted him on the shoulder.

Later, I heard Mr. Cavan confiding to Da, "In my own home I am unwanted. His mother fawns over him, and the two of them treat me with disdain."

The men went off to an undesignated place where guns were hidden, and to a quiet, vacant field where they could practice firing.

When Da, Donal and Fingal returned late that night, I was waiting up. They settled themselves by candlelight, their faces ruddy with the wind. I poured steaming tea into their cups, then sliced a soda loaf and set it before them.

"I'd like to learn to fire the gun," I said plainly as I faced them, ready to argue if I had to. In the hours that they'd been gone, I had thought of all the reasons I should know how to shoot.

"No, for the love of all that's holy!" Da cried.

I could see by the expression on Donal's face that he didn't think it such a bad idea, and maybe that was what made me even bolder. "I am often here alone caring for Mam and Ishleen," I said.

"Be practical, Da," Donal said. "You don't like the idea of your daughter with a gun, but she needs it without us here. The English might come and you might not be home. I want to teach her."

Donal took something wrapped in cloth out of a satchel and, laying it on the table slowly, ceremoniously unraveled it. He explained to me exactly how it worked, and promised that in the morning he would take me out to the field and teach me to shoot.

But very early the next morning, Emmet Leahy arrived and said they had to leave immediately, that he had received word of English soldiers on a road they'd planned to take. Now they'd have to head a different, longer way.

"Da will teach you to shoot, Maeve," Donal said.

It was a rushed goodbye, my brothers shuffling to get things, hardly awake and with no time even for a cup of tea.

"I'm proud of both of you, my sons!" Da said, though all the color had gone from his face. We watched them move swiftly down the hill, following Emmet Leahy and two other men.

That day, Da took the boat out on the water alone. Ishleen and I watched him staring at Woman's Crag, lost in thought. For the first time, he looked fragile, as if the mist might swallow him.

This made me even more anxious to learn how to shoot, but I knew I'd have a devil of a time getting Da to teach me.

That afternoon, an east wind blew in milder temperatures, and Ishleen, Mam and I went to the shore. As I pushed Mam's wheeled chair, Ishleen carried two creels, one for each of us to collect the blue-black mussels from where they clustered on the rocks.

Tom Cavan appeared out of nowhere, standing a few yards off on the sand, the tails of his sky-blue coat rippling in the wind as he watched us.

"Maeve," he said. "I want to talk to you."

"What is it?" I asked warily.

"Over here," he said, beckoning to me.

I stood up and started walking over to him.

He moved toward me suddenly and grabbed my arm.

"Stop it!" I cried, struggling free of him.

His eyes narrowed, and he was fuming a little. He had grown so much larger in the last few years, and I was afraid of how strong he was. I wondered, too, about the mysterious life his father said he led. "The only sensible thing for us is to marry," he said.

"No," I said firmly, and walked back toward the rocks, but he rushed after me and blocked my way.

"Your brothers are gone and your father is old. You've no one to protect you. It's natural that we marry. In the end it will come to that."

"It won't come to that," I said calmly.

Ishleen peered angrily at Tom, who remained where he was.

"What are you looking at, you odd little thing? You know your own mother is the way she is because of you!"

Ishleen lowered her head and squinted in the mild sunlight, Tom's words piercing her.

It was the way he looked at Mam's vacant form with an air of triumph that made me think again of what I'd felt before, that he was somehow responsible for what had happened to her.

"I'd never marry you, Tom Cavan," I said gravely. "Never!"

He took in a deep breath. "You'll have nothing left, soon enough, Maeve O'Tullagh, and your hand will be forced. You should start getting used to the idea."

He refused to leave, so Ishleen and I packed up our baskets.

On the way up the hill, Ishleen asked me to tell her about Mam when she had still walked and spoke.

"She could feel you wanting to be born," I said. "You were trying so hard to be with Mam."

Ishleen looked at me, her wild nimbus of hair glinting in the sunlight.

"Do you remember? Do you remember wanting to be born?"

"I remember something," she said. "A place."

I stopped pushing Mam's chair. "What was the place like?"

"Very cold and windy. The walls and floors were made of ice."

"I think it's where Mam's soul is, Ishleen."

I described the vast room I kept envisioning, with its white and pale blue embellished walls, iced over, and the blasts of wind blowing sparkles of frost.

"Yes, Maeve. I remember that room."

"Do you know where that place is, Ishleen?" I pleaded.

She shook her head helplessly. "I only know it's very cold there."

We scaled the hill, and when we were safe inside the cottage, I knelt down in front of her. "Oh, Ishleen," I said. "If you could just try to remember something more about that place."

"I'll try, Maeve," she said.

I went to the hearth and blew on the embers, and small flames appeared from the ashes. Ishleen gazed at them in earnest, as if they might jog some old memory.

"It's cold there. Very cold. I wanted to leave."

But try as we both did to find any other clues, all that Ishleen could remember was the cold and that particular iced-over room. And all we could do to quell our frustrations over Mam was embrace and kiss her, comb her hair and pamper the vacant body still with us.

It wasn't a fortnight before we got a letter from my brothers.

Donal wrote:

> The Irish are naturals at subterfuge. Our plans
> are very carefully made, and I believe we will
> be successful. And I have news on another
> exciting front. King Philip the second is
> preparing a fleet to battle the English in Irish
> waters. The Spaniards in such large number and

so well armed as they are will definitely weaken
the English and greatly reduce their threat to the
Irish people.

Tom Cavan stayed in Ard Macha, and even though I sometimes saw him watching Ishleen and me from a distance when we drove the cows, we managed to avoid him. I had the sense that he was thinking hard about something, trying to decide his next move.

Sometimes Ishleen and I noticed a front of mist on the sea past Woman's Crag, more visible in the hours when the daylight was waning. It was not like a regular curtain of mist rising off the water, because it seemed to locate itself in one area.

One dusk as I was taking our clothes in off the line, I looked down at the sea. The mist was whiter and denser than I'd ever seen it. It parted very slightly in one area, revealing a shiver of twinkling lights, then closed again immediately. As the sky darkened, the mist became indiscernible.

The next evening Ishleen and I went out to look for the curtain of mist, but it seemed to have vanished.

Part Two

The Spanish Ships

CHAPTER 10

Donal and Fingal had been gone almost two months when a violent September storm raged along the coast and a Spanish ship hit Woman's Crag. Then, fighting stiff southwesterly headwinds, the boat turned toward the shore of the mainland and, trying to beach itself, was wrecked in the jagged rocks of the coast.

An hour before it happened, Mr. Cavan had told us he had heard talk of English soldiers in Killybegs, just south of the ford. For more than a week, people had been whispering about the Spaniards that had come in fleets of ships to help the Irish drive out the English. But the Spanish had been defeated right away in the southeast waters on the other side of Ireland. The retreating Spanish ships took the long course all the way to the north, rounding the head of Donegal, and continuing south along our western coast toward Spain. The weather had been against them, the seas tumultuous and unpredictable.

Da, who'd lived four decades on this storm coast, said he'd never seen such violent, heartbreaking weather.

Wearing oilcloth coats and boots, Ishleen and I followed Da and Mr. Cavan to stand in the driving wet and look at the great galleon, its sails shredded and beating madly at the masts.

"Something devilish about it," Da said, squinting into the wind, his face streaked with rain.

"A death ship," Mr. Cavan yelled over the noise of wind and sea. "Surely its fate is already written."

"God help them!" my father cried, and made the sign of the cross. As the ship hit more rocks, there was a loud, slow crashing noise.

Da and Mr. Cavan made their way down to the beach in the storm to see the ship still trying to approach our precipitous shoreline. It was filling with water, leaning heavily to one side, and fires had started within the hull in places not deluged with rain. The ship's name, emblazoned on its side in calligraphic letters, was *Nuestra Señora de la Soledad.*

The Spaniards began to jump from their ship into the water. The waves lifted them high and low, and it was terrible to see how the water dashed them against the rocks. Ishleen and I embraced hard and hunched near the rocky hillside, holding our own against the wind. Some of the dead came in on the tide while others remained facedown on the water's back, lifting and dropping, going under and appearing again.

My father and Mr. Cavan took their boats out, nearly losing their own lives trying to rescue any man still living.

Mrs. Cavan stood on the cliff above, her shawl and skirts beating wildly in the wind. Tom appeared suddenly behind her, peering down at me and Ishleen.

Among the dozens of Spaniards struggling to come ashore that day, only three survived.

Mr. Cavan enlisted a reluctant Tom to help bring the injured Spaniards up to their house. Mrs. Cavan had set a big pallet on the floor, and the men were laid there. Ishleen and I helped Mrs. Cavan go to work on the men's injuries while my father and Mr. Cavan took turns keeping an eye out for English soldiers. But they both came back in when the weather got too bad to stay outside. The wind howled like twenty banshees, and Ishleen clung to me, pressing her face against my stomach and squeezing her eyes shut. The Cavans' cottage, which had always seemed rooted to the limestone of Ard Macha, shook as if it might be lifted onto the back of the wind.

"When the storm quiets, the English will come," my father said. "They'll see that wreck out there and all the dead, and they'll come up here looking for any still alive."

"Yes," Mr. Cavan said. "And the devils'll shoot the

Spaniards on sight. We should be hiding them as soon as the winds calm." He pulled aside a curtain and pointed to an area where their sow and her seven piglets were weathering the storm.

Tom, who was standing in the shadows, spoke suddenly. "What will the English do if they know we're helping the Spaniards?"

My father and Mr. Cavan exchanged a glance. "They'd likely arrest us, but with your help, Tom, we'll be driving the sow and her sucklings out of the little side room and hiding these men in there, and they'll never have to know."

Ishleen and I tore fabric for the men's wounds. Two of them were unconscious, but one who could not have been much older than me kept opening and closing his eyes, as if he were in the middle of a terrible dream he was trying to awaken from. He mumbled and cried out, moving his head from side to side. He had black hair and thick, expressive eyebrows. On one ear he wore a small gold earring.

"Shhh," I whispered, kneeling over him. Very gently I pushed the damp black hair away from his forehead and neck, and dabbed his skin with cool water. His eyes opened suddenly, and as he looked at me, he spoke in a fierce whisper, *"Todos están muertos. Todo mis amigos."*

Though I did not understand his words, the power of the grief in the sound of them caused a quake of emotion to rush through me like a wave. He winced against his pain and his eyelids fluttered, and soon he closed them again, breathing and moving feverishly. I felt stunned, and remained there kneeling over him, wanting desperately to know what it was he'd said so that I could help quell his suffering somehow. I watched his lips as he mumbled, and saw something flash between two of his teeth: a small bright red jewel embedded there, probably a ruby.

Something made me turn. Tom was watching us with narrowed hawklike eyes. And so I moved away from the Spaniard and tried to behave casually, busying myself by stoking the fire. Da and Mr. Cavan brought the sow and her piglets into the main area of the cottage, and carefully moved the injured soldiers into the side room.

When the wind quieted, about half an hour later, Tom slipped outside. For a while, I struggled to stay calm, but feeling nervous about what he might be up to, I went out.

A swarm of English soldiers in red tarps was on the beach below, inspecting the dead and the ruined ship. Tom stood among them, talking and pointing up the cliff.

I ran back to the cottage, threw the door open, and shouted, "Tom's speaking to the English soldiers! And I saw him pointing up here!"

"Christ, could that creature be my own son?" Mr. Cavan cried out, and Mrs. Cavan shot him an angry look.

Within minutes, four soldiers arrived. "We know you're hiding Spaniards in this cottage," one of them said. He was an imposing figure with a barrel chest and a coat much too tight for him. His big red face was streaming with rain. He looked around the place with squinting eyes, and sneered as if disgusted.

Pointing at the sow in the corner, he asked my father, "Is that your wife?" My father's face went purple, and his jaw tightened. His hands became fists, but I saw him close his eyes and resist his impulse to hit the man. In that moment, tense with anger and restraint, my father's muscles looked like they were made of iron.

The red-faced man stepped forward and moved the curtain aside, revealing the injured Spaniards.

The soldiers arrested my father and Mr. Cavan and took them to Dungarven, while a younger soldier, fair-haired with small cold eyes and a scar on his chin, took the three surviving Spaniards outside and shot them in the rain.

The rain kept on that evening. Ishleen and I went home, nervous that Tom might return. We were fretting over our father and kept looking anxiously outside.

Rain was pouring hard, but I ventured out onto the road again and again, once going as far as the place where the Spanish soldiers had been shot. That was when I saw one of them move, the young black-haired one with the ruby in his tooth. I stood there holding the hood of my tarp over my head, watching, hardly breathing, and he moved again.

My heart raced. I ran down to where he lay and knelt beside him. The rain had pooled in his ear and around the lids of his closed eyes. He opened his mouth and seemed to be trying to drink the rain. I could see the wound on his shoulder where he'd been shot. I struggled to wake him, his eyes squinting against the wet. After much cajoling, I managed to get him to his feet.

Something fell from one of his pockets, and I picked it up. It was a small compass made of pewter, the sensitive needle under the glass window moving wildly, like something alive and in a panic. Decoratively carved within its window were words I assumed were Spanish and could not translate; just above those, I was stunned to see a tiny, delicate rendering of the triple spiral.

Not believing my eyes, I wiped the beading droplets of rain from the compass with the inside of my sleeve and examined the design. It was unmistakenly the triple spiral. Very gingerly I returned the compass to his pocket.

He leaned heavily on me as I brought him home, where I tended to his shoulder, using my father's whiskey to clean it. His bloodstained shirt was in shreds, so I carefully removed it and helped him into one of Da's warm shirts of heavy woven cloth, the color of oats.

I gave him some water to drink and offered him food, and though he tried, he could barely stomach it.

CHAPTER 11

he storm continued to rage throughout the night. The next day, I left little precocious Ishleen watching over Mam and the wounded Spaniard while I stole from the house, leaning into the wet wind and finding my way to Mrs. Cavan's. She had no word of my father or her husband.

"How could Tom have done such a thing, Mrs. Cavan, to his own father and to mine?"

"There's bad blood between Tom and his father," she said.

"I'm very worried. He's said to me that soon I'll have nothing and that I'll have to marry him. Is that what he's up to, turning my father over to the English?" I grabbed her hard by the wrist and looked into her face. "If my father is hurt in any way at all, I will curse Tom's name to my grave! I'd rather move to Galway and beg in the streets. He doesn't know who I am if he thinks he can reduce me to nothing and then win me."

Mrs. Cavan looked as though I'd hit her in the stomach. "I will tell him, Maeve. I think if he believes it might bring you round to him, he'll do the opposite and make sure your father stays safe. The fact is, for whatever reason, it's you he wants to marry."

I was about to rush out when she called me back.

"Maeve, if he does that for you—brings your father back, I mean—will you accept his offer?"

"I cannot promise you. All I can say is that if my father is not returned safely to Ard Macha, my hatred for your son will never be soothed."

She nodded and ushered me out the door. As she did, she told me that she had seen another Spanish ship at dawn, passing unsteadily in the storm, and had spoken to neighbors from the valley who'd told her that four or five other Spanish ships fighting stiff southwesterly headwinds had crashed along the jagged coastlines to the south. And the English, distracted by those ships and traveling there in droves to meet and execute any survivors, were leaving us temporarily alone.

When I returned, Ishleen told me that the Spaniard had sat up and had drunk some water and eaten a little bread. Now he was asleep again in the box bed, the curtain drawn around him. As I told Ishleen what Mrs. Cavan had said, the Spaniard moaned. We went to him, pulling the curtain aside. He arched his long neck backward, squeezing his eyes closed. His dark skin glistened with sweat. We knelt beside him and wondered what to do for him.

"The poor creature," I whispered.

I couldn't help but notice how beautifully formed he was, even in his distress. His black hair lay thick on the pillow, and I touched it softly, astonished by its silken texture. Trying to comfort him, I combed it with my fingers, and this quieted him a little. The jewel between his teeth flashed each time he winced with pain.

Ishleen began to sing to him, something she sometimes sang to Mam, an old Irish song about the gentle breezes that will come from the west: *"Tioctaidh an le-outhne bhog aniar."* Though he did not open his eyes, he quieted and seemed more at peace. Then she sang a song about June sunshine on the grass: *"Grian an Mheithimh in ullghort."* His sleep grew peaceful.

I sat near the hearth and sighed, feeling my own exhaustion. Lulled by Ishleen's voice, I closed my eyes.

I don't know how long I slept there sitting up, but when I awakened, the Spaniard was leaning on one elbow, his eyes fixed upon me. For a moment I stared back without moving. His eyes were dark brown, radiant with flecks of amber.

Ishleen, who had been pouring water from a pitcher on the other side of the hearth, approached excitedly and handed the Spaniard a cup of water. With shaking hands he took the cup and drank. Then he sat up and, leaning his legs over the side of the bed, hunched forward, breathing with effort. The pain he was feeling seemed to make him angry. He gritted his teeth and squeezed his eyes shut.

"¡Ay, maldiga los ingleses!" He spit the words. "Maldígalos al infierno."

After a moment, he raised his face and looked at the two of us. He pointed to his chest and said, "Francisco."

I pointed to myself and said, "Maeve," then to my sister. "Ishleen." I looked at Mam where she sat in a shadow near the loft stair. Her head hung forward. Guilty for having ignored her all this time, I went to her, lifting her head gently and pushing her wheeled chair into the dim lamplight.

The hard spatter of rain intensified, and the wind shook the foundation of the house. "This is my—" I began, but before I could finish, there was a loud knock on the door, and the three of us looked at one another fearfully.

"Maybe it's Da," Ishleen whispered.

"I hope so," I said, "but just in case, both of you stay back here behind the curtain." I pulled the curtain closed around them and made an urgent gesture, not knowing how much Irish Francisco understood.

I opened the door only a little to see Tom Cavan's face peering at me from under his hood, the wind causing his coat to flap and pull, like it might fly off his very body.

"Let me in, Maeve," he yelled, "out of this weather!"

"No, Tom," I said firmly. "How dare you come here after what you've done. To do such a thing to your own father, and to mine!"

I tried to close the door, but he pushed against it.

"One of the Spaniards that was shot is gone. He might be a danger. I'm here to protect you lest he come here. Let me in!"

"You're more of a danger than a wounded man who is likely starving to death, Tom Cavan! Now go, and leave my sister and mother and me in peace!"

"Maeve, I'm going to try to help your father. I'm going to bring him home."

"You should, since it is because of you that he's in English custody."

He looked frustrated by my refusal to let him in, and pushed harder against the door. Panicking, I redoubled my effort against him. He glowered at me, and I thought for certain he would now overpower me, but he surprised me by stepping back. His expression as he did so was somewhere between determined and perplexed, and I thought of the conversation I'd had with his mother. She had clearly persuaded him not to force my hand.

I closed and bolted the door and stayed near it, listening until I heard his retreating footsteps through the storm.

I joined Ishleen and Francisco behind the curtain. Francisco was still sitting up, breathing with effort. In spite of the cold air in the room, droplets of sweat ran down his temples. He sighed heavily, then hunched forward, giving himself over to his thoughts, as if recalling terrible things. He grew distressed, as he'd been while dreaming.

It occurred to me that he was the only survivor of *Nuestra Señora de la Soledad.*

We remained in silence for a while, waiting for our hearts to settle again. Ishleen lifted the cup of water, offering it to him, but Francisco touched his stomach and gestured putting a spoon to his mouth.

"He's hungry!" Ishleen said. I got up and put some leftover porridge on the fire. Francisco's eyes followed me in every move I made, and I could not tell if this caused me to be more excited or more nervous. My heart was racing and my cheeks felt hot.

I poured milk into the pot with the porridge and stirred it over the flame. As I cooked, I turned and caught him staring at me. Our eyes locked, and I found myself unable to look away.

If there hadn't been such pain in his expression, I'd have called his steady look too bold. Yet, at the same time, a shiver of mysterious affection filled me, as if he were someone well known to me. With effort, I blinked and turned away, but even then, the dark beauty of his face remained, imprinted on my field of vision. It mattered so little, perhaps not at all, that I could not understand his language.

If I could have spoken to him, the thing I would have told him, as odd as it seemed in those dangerous moments, was about the dress of delicate metal and the room with the iced-over walls and the gusts of wind. And that if I could only find that place, I might bring Mam back.

It was just at this moment that I glanced over at Mam, and Francisco also turned and peered into the shadow where she sat. He gazed at her for a few seconds, then looked back at me.

"Your . . . *madre*? Mother?" he asked.

I nodded, my heart sinking for poor Mam.

He watched my eyes. His expression, worn from exhaustion and grief, was so unguarded that I was pierced by a multitude of sensations and a yearning of the same nature that I often felt gazing into the western sea. I looked away from him, stirring the oats until they were of a good consistency, then ladled a dish full.

Ishleen and I watched with absorption as Francisco ate. He stopped once as he was raising the spoon to his mouth, looked at us, and a half smile broke onto his face. Everything about his handsome visage came into intense focus with that smile, which was skewed to one side of his mouth. A long dimple scored each cheek, and his eyes glimmered.

When he finished eating, he approached Mam, focusing on the triple spiral around her neck. I touched his arm and showed him the one Ishleen wore with the little bottle attached to it. Francisco looked closely at it, as if in awe. For the last year or so, Ishleen had no longer needed the bottle sewn into her clothes for safekeeping, and now wore it as a necklace.

"You have?" he asked, and pointed at my neck. I shook my head. Then he pointed to his jacket, which I had laid near the fire to dry. He went over to it, opened it, and showed me the compass with the triple spiral.

He looked again in Mam's direction, then went to his

knees. He touched the spiral, and it hummed, so Ishleen and I looked at each other. For a moment, Mam's breathing became audible.

Noticing this, he whispered, *"Señora, regrese a nosotros."*

A certain effervescence came into her posture, and, though I was afraid to believe it, I thought I saw more light in her eyes.

I got on my knees beside him and took Mam's hands, searching her face. Very gradually the little bit of renewed life faded. Still, as I knelt there, a flicker of hope caused me to shiver. Francisco, having grown tired, now hung his head and breathed with effort. He got up, dragged himself back to the bed, and lay carefully down, wincing as he did. He sighed and half closed his eyes.

I pulled the curtain around him, then looked at Ishleen, who was peering excitedly at me.

"What do the three spirals mean, Maeve?" she asked.

"I don't know, Ishleen, but it's something we have in common with Francisco."

In the middle of the night, there was a loud banging on the door. I bolted to my feet, and Ishleen sat up. "Maeve!" She gave me a frightened look.

The fire had gone down to a few red embers in the white ash.

Francisco drew aside the curtain.

"No," I whispered, shaking my head.

The banging began again, and a deep, unfamiliar male voice shouted, "Open, or I'll shoot the lock away!"

"English!" Ishleen whispered.

I suddenly remembered the gun Donal had left for Da. I went to my knees and, moving the hearthstone aside, drew it out. I'd held it before, but was alarmed now at how heavy it was.

Even though Da had never followed through and taught me to use the gun, I recalled the things Donal had said the night he'd explained its workings to me.

"Donal said it has bullets," Ishleen whispered.

The soldier pounded again. "Open!"

Holding the gun behind me in my left hand, I opened the door. The sudden bright beam of a lamp pierced the shadows of the room. It was the soldier with the scar on his chin, the one who had shot Francisco and his two friends. He gave me an impatient cursory glance, obviously thinking I was no threat, and pushed in past me, his eyes on the curtain Ishleen was standing in front of.

Sensing that she was hiding someone, he pushed Ishleen out of the way and drew the curtain aside, so roughly that part of it tore.

He aimed his gun, and I saw his finger move obliquely toward the trigger. With lightning speed I pointed Donal's gun at his back and shot.

Time got stuck then in a long, distended moment. The soldier froze, dropping the lamp, which landed on its side on the floor. Incapacitated, his mouth hung open and his eyes bulged in utter shock. Then, at last, he fell.

Shaking violently, I put the gun down and picked up the lamp.

Francisco came out from behind the curtain and squatted beside the soldier. He took the gun from the soldier's hand and examined it, turning a cartridge and looking inside, counting the bullets.

Everything we did from that moment on happened quickly. Wincing, Francisco was on his feet, laying a blanket on the ground. The three of us coaxed and rolled and pushed the soldier's body until he lay on the blanket. While Ishleen stayed with Mam with the door bolted, Francisco and I hauled the body down to the beach, Francisco stopping now and again and breathing with difficulty.

A muted moon was just visible through the starlit clouds, and though it was still raining, there was a reprieve in its intensity.

We laid the soldier's body close to the cold tide, which rushed in with purposeful momentum, pushing and pulling at him, trying to claim him.

Francisco headed for the cliff, but I remained near the dead soldier, looking at his face, which the vague moon dimly illuminated. He was a young man. In death, no threat left in him, he had a soft, childlike expression. A bolt of remorse shook me.

Francisco approached and took my arm gently, his dark eyes catching the moonlight and turning it faintly amber.

Sensing his gratitude, I shivered inwardly and reminded myself that if I had not shot the soldier, he would have killed Francisco. Francisco's eyes made me feel strong, my heart beating high in my chest. I imagined the soft metal dress and saw myself storming the icy, elegant room.

Francisco looked at me as if he wished to convey something, but sighed. Perhaps he had not been able to find the words in my language. He touched my shoulder with his warm hand.

"*Vamos,*" he said in a quiet voice, and took my hand, leading me away from the dead soldier. "Your mama, your sister." He pointed toward the cottage.

"You know some words in Irish," I said.

He held his thumb and forefinger half an inch apart. "Irish," he said. "*Poquito.* Little."

Lightning flashed in the sky, and a warm metallic smell filled the wet air. Moments later, thunder cracked and rumbled, and a new belt of heavy rain moved in over Ard Macha.

Back in the cottage, I was still shaking as we dried off. I gave Francisco some of Da's clothes to wear and struggled to think of a safe place where we could go and hide.

Ishleen helped me put things into a satchel: several blocks of turf and matches, a sack of oats and half a loaf of soda bread, ten potatoes, a turnip, and the bottle of whiskey.

The wheeled chair was no good to us where we were going, through sand and jagged rocks and tidewater.

Francisco and Ishleen took Mam's arms, guiding her, and followed as I led the way down the hill carrying the supplies.

CHAPTER 12

To the south along the beach, under the limestone overhang where Da and my brothers used to fish for black pollack, there was a system of natural corridors that opened into a cave, deep enough in the wall of rock that a burning fire could not be seen from any passing boats. Because of the jutting nature of the headland, we lay completely hidden, a haven from anyone on shore.

We slept there that night, though I could hardly call it sleep. My mind was in a daze, reliving the noise of the gun and the way it had shaken and deafened me, the face of the soldier in the rain and the tide.

In the daylight, we came down from the cave and stood on the stones where my father and brothers used to fish. Hard rain still fell, and gales blew, and when it all quieted a little, a mist descended so that we could see no horizon between sea and sky.

Mam remained half sitting, propped up against a blanket in the cave. I led Francisco inside and gestured for him to go near her, and speak to her as he had the night before. He squatted down and whispered to her in Spanish. I saw again, with a racing heart, a subtle effervescent light encasing Mam, her eyes stirring faintly as if with memory. Ishleen and I watched breathlessly, but soon, as if the energy and faint animation were too difficult to maintain, the barely visible twinkling light fled all at once.

Francisco gritted his teeth and closed his eyes, his hand hovering near the gunshot wound. I told him that I should clean it. He sat down on the ground. My hands shook as I carefully removed the makeshift bandage. I dabbed a cloth with whiskey and cleansed the gash in his skin. He winced, squeezing his eyes shut hard.

When it was finished, Francisco stood and sighed, then went back out and wandered a few yards away. He sat on a shelf of rock with his arms wrapped around his bent legs, resting his face on his knees.

The tide filled the pools between rocks with pollack and skate. I had brought a fishing pole, and while Ishleen sat with her legs dangling off the rock, catching fish, I stole glances at Francisco, who brooded there, staring down into the dark water.

At dusk, the splatter of the rain on the sea took on a soothing, almost hypnotic sound. The mood of the weather had gone from violent to soft. I built a fire and cooked the fish Ishleen had caught. We all ate, and then she went into the cave, where Mam was still propped up. Ishleen laid her head on Mam's lap and fell into a deep, exhausted sleep.

The descending sun burned red in the humid sky, cleared of clouds. Francisco and I went south past the rocks to a long strand of beach, an unfamiliar stretch that looked like an alien country in the red light of the waning day.

Big pieces of Francisco's wrecked ship bobbed and rocked on the waves, with some bits stuck in the sand or the rocks. As we approached, I was stunned to see the tide washing over a giant figure of a woman wrapped in kelp. We ran to it and discovered the twelve-foot-tall figurehead from the front of his ship.

"Nuestra Señora de la Soledad," he said.

"What does it mean?" I asked.

"Nuestra Señora . . . ," he began. " 'Our Lady.' "

I nodded.

". . . de la Soledad," he continued, and hung his head, searching his mind for the word that might translate it best.

" 'Alone,' " he said.

"Our Lady Alone? Lonely?"

He shook his head. *"Soledad,"* he said softly, then looked at me and said enthusiastically, " 'Solitude'!"

"Our Lady of Solitude," I said thoughtfully, and studied her. I cleared her damp polished face of seaweed, then ran one hand over her prominent cheekbone. Her mouth was the same shape as Mam's, lips pressed closed and tense at the corners. Her wide open eyes were set upon something that no one but she saw. She was a giant beauty, but petrified in her eternal longing, seeing nothing but the thing missing from her.

Walking down the length of her supine body, I studied the gracefully carved hands, both pressed to her heart. At the bottom of her dull rose-colored dress, the wood was fractured in places; salt had gathered there and glistened white like streaks of snow.

Francisco gestured for me to help him bring her up from the water. With effort, we dragged her farther up the beach and stood her, impaling the broken wood beneath her hem as deep as we could into the sand. She towered over us, a monument leaning toward the western sea, facing the waves.

"She's looking toward the Holy Isles," I said, pointing at the horizon.

He nodded, understanding immediately what I had said. *"Las Santas Islas,"* he said.

He brought out his compass and showed it to me. The Spanish words that I'd seen there before were *Las Santas Islas.*

Instead of north being the top of the four compass points, west was. The face of the compass was embellished in places with Celtic knots.

I marveled that he, too, knew of the Holy Isles, and I remembered what Emmet Leahy had said about the ancient intimacy between the Irish and the Spanish. The triple spiral, I realized with wonderment, was connected somehow to the Holy Isles.

"I used to dream of sailing in search of the Holy Isles," I said.

He nodded. "*Peligroso* . . . dangerous journey."

"But beautiful," I said.

"*Sí*."

He tapped his forehead with his finger. "Maybe only *islas* . . . isles in the mind. *El sueño de un niño*. The dream . . . of a child." He stared darkly toward the horizon, where the sun was still descending, causing the sky to burn very red and the streaks of gold to go purple. Gulls flew at all altitudes, cawing mercilessly above us.

"I believe in the isles," I said, and touched my chest, nodding, in case he didn't understand. "I think they are there."

I handed him back his compass, and as his arm brushed against mine, my heart gave a little jump.

He noticed this and looked at me thoughtfully, then came close, a tender flinch in his eye. He touched my hair, sweeping a strand away from my face. I felt a kind of vertigo, as if I might fall, but in slow motion.

He embraced me and held me close to him so that I could feel his strong heart beating against my neck. Closing my eyes, I felt myself melting into him, drifting into some other state of being, in which every pulse in my body tolled like a bell. After such upheaval, the world was recovering itself with a heightened intensity. The wind rose and fell, deepening some moments to a high chorus, then fading into silence.

In that hour, as the sun disappeared and left the sky

dark blue, it was as if we were utterly alone on the planet, with only Mam and Ishleen safely dreaming in the nearby cave, the giant lady of solitude presiding over us.

It was dark when we crept back to the cave. I took my place beside the slumbering Ishleen, and he took his place on the other side of the fire, which was almost out. A few times as I started to sleep, I opened my eyes and looked over at him in the light of the dying embers. His eyes were open and he stared into the darkness above him.

In the middle of the night I heard soft voices. Both Francisco and Ishleen were deep asleep. I got up and crept out through the corridor to the threshold, following the sounds.

The water was very still, the sky above, clear and wildly starry, and each star's reflection shimmered on the water's surface, a quiet festival of lights.

On the shelf of rock where Francisco had sat in a reverie earlier in the day were two figures wearing purple jackets with silver braiding—the uniform of the crew of *Nuestra Señora de la Soledad,* the same jacket Francisco wore. At first I could make out only their silhouettes and minimal movements, but the wet silver braiding issued a faint illuminated mist that rose like steam from their shoulders. I did not breathe, and gradually my eyes adjusted enough that I could see that the two young men were dark-haired like Francisco. They whispered and conferred excitedly with each other.

One of them saw me and informed the other one and they froze where they were. For some reason that I did not understand, I knew that they were dead or no longer of the world Francisco, Ishleen and I lived in. And then I realized why. They were the other two rescued Spaniards, Francisco's friends who had died when they'd been shot.

The one who had seen me first took off his jacket, leaving it on the rock. His human silhouette lost its contours and he became a dark liquid shadow that poured itself into the water. The other one followed suit. When the water they had disappeared into had gone quiet again, I looked at the jackets that lay on the rock, sleeves in expressive postures still steaming, the wet silver cording ignited.

I looked out at the sea. It must have been filled with the Spanish dead, yet the elements seemed to be rejoicing and excited, in the way the two Spaniards had been before they'd seen me. Shouldn't the sea feel like a giant tomb, I wondered, floating with Spaniards and a single murdered Englishman? Instead there was a shivery animation to the new silence and the starlight, a charge on the air and an exhilaration barely held in check. I thought of Francisco sleeping inside, and my heart quickened. He seemed like the single survivor of a dark-haired breed of gods. Maybe he'd been meant for the sea as well, but Ishleen and Mam and I were keeping him, holding him in this other world.

When I looked again at the shelf of rock, the two jackets were gone.

A few minutes later, Francisco appeared at the threshold of the cave, carrying the lamp, looking questioningly at me.

I hesitated, then said, "Seals. I was watching them swim."

He raised his eyebrows and smiled, then exclaimed in a soft voice, "Seals! They are . . ." He struggled to find words. "Humans."

"Like humans?" I asked.

Ishleen came out then, rubbing her eyes sleepily.

Suddenly, as if it were a vision, a Spanish boat appeared, an armada ship. *"La Hermana de la Luna!"* Francisco cried, and held up the lamp, waving his arms wildly at them.

The ship dropped anchor. With the water so calm and the moon so bright, the sailors could see the rockiness of the beach and knew not to attempt to come closer. Two men boarded a small boat and were lowered to the water. They navigated between the rocks and came toward us as Francisco ran anxiously into the sea. He and the Spaniards spoke in urgent tones to one another.

Ishleen ran back into the cave and came out with the soda loaf. She stood on the rock shelf and waved it, offering it to them. The small boat came in close, and one of the Spaniards accepted it, but he did not seem worn with hunger the way Francisco had been, and their boat looked much less battered, regal even as it waited there on the clear horizon, sailors watching from deck. Francisco pointed to the ship's carved figurehead of a young woman leaning seaward, her dark hair the same length as mine. Straining forward from the stern, her forearms extended and palms facing up, her posture and her entire bearing suggested that she was on a kind of noble quest.

"*La Hermana de la Luna.* 'The Sister of the Moon,' " he said.

"She looks like Maeve," Ishleen said.

Francisco looked at it again and then at me, and nodded in acknowledgment.

"*Vamos,*" the Spaniard said to Francisco.

I panicked, thinking of Mam inside and how I was sure Francisco could bring her back to life.

"No! Don't go!" I cried out.

Francisco locked eyes with me, and we stood facing each other waist-deep in the bay, steadying ourselves against the gentle surges of the waves.

"*¡Vamos!*" he said. "Come."

I looked at Ishleen. "Let's bring Mam and go with him."

"No, Maeve!" Ishleen said. "We can't leave Da!"

I knew she was right. I looked at Francisco with pained reluctance, and shook my head.

He came in close, pressed his mouth to my ear and whispered, "*Gracias.*"

A shiver ran the length of me.

I closed my eyes and felt his lips on my temple. He let go and stepped back from me, leaving me with racing pulses.

Francisco looked at his fellow sailor and said something

fast in Spanish. The sailor looked at me and said, "He says he comes back for you one day soon."

"Promise," I said.

"Promise," Francisco repeated.

He was about to get into the little boat when something occurred to him. He unbuttoned his purple jacket and handed it to me, nodding that I should take it. I thought of the ghost Spaniards wearing their wet jackets on the stone. It seemed an ill omen, but he urged me.

He came close again, nodding very definitively. "*Por favor,* Maeve. You please keep me *vivo.*"

I pressed the coat close to my chest as he climbed into the boat.

I looked to the other sailor. "*Vivo?*" I asked.

"It means . . . *alive,*" the sailor answered.

I held the jacket to my chest and watched as the little boat met the big ship. Several men helped Francisco on board and greeted him with embraces. A distinctive-looking man among them, tall and very thin, with wild black hair, looked out at Ishleen and me wistfully and waved.

I remained in the water watching until *La Hermana de la Luna* disappeared on the southern horizon.

CHAPTER 13

With Francisco gone, Ishleen and I led Mam slowly back to Ard Macha, and were overjoyed to find Da returned from Dungarven.

Old Peig was there with him. She told us that when she'd heard that he'd come home and found an empty house, she'd worried and come to look after him. They were both greatly relieved to see us and shocked by the tale I had to tell.

Da was despondent and tired. He sat that night before the fire, and Old Peig, who said she'd stay on with us for a while, pampered him as best as she could, but he refused to talk about his days in English captivity. And when we asked about Mr. Cavan, he shook his head. He told us that Tom Cavan was responsible for getting him freed, but the shameful thing was that he had done nothing to help his own father.

Old Peig told us that the day after Tom Cavan had seen to it that Da was sent home, he'd disappeared again from Ard Macha.

The next morning, soft weather returned, skies gray and lightly damp with rain. I insisted that Da let Ishleen and me come out to fish with him.

One hour felt like five hours, rocking in the boat on the sea. The misty weather was a kind of limbo in which we remained suspended, and sitting for so long on the cold water, the gloom had a way of getting into the soul.

I daydreamed about the storm's violence, and the way it had ended in brilliant calm. My eyes were always on the horizon to the south, where *La Hermana de la Luna* had disappeared.

That afternoon, I restlessly wandered as far as the edge of Dungarven, looking for any news at all about the Spanish ships, but no one knew a thing, only vague reports about armada wrecks to the south. I told myself that the ship Francisco was on had been undamaged, that the men had seemed healthy, and these factors increased the possibility that they would survive.

The news I did come by was not what I'd been hoping to hear. Emmet Leahy, my brothers and two other men were fugitives, running and hiding from the English for having set fire to one of their camps.

I went home and reluctantly told this to Da.

* * *

I sat with Mam that evening, whispering to her, rubbing her hands between both of mine to warm them. And try as I did to search her face for the reassuring spark of life that had appeared when Francisco had spoken to her, I could not find it. She looked like a drowned woman.

"*Señora,*" I whispered to her softly, the way Francisco had. I struggled to remember other Spanish words but could only remember the names of the ships. "*Nuestra Señora de la Soledad,*" I added, and then remembered what it meant.

I watched for even a faint rush of blood to her cheek, a glimmer to return to her eyes.

"Please, Mam," I whispered. "Please." But the skin of her brow, her eyelids and her mouth all looked heavier and cooler than I had ever seen them.

I wrapped Mam in Francisco's jacket, hoping she might sense him through it. I warmed the cold metal buttons against my palm, traced the intricacies of the silver braiding with my fingertips and memorized the thick seams and their contours. Mam's arms got lost in the long sleeves.

In a delirium, I breathed traces of his sweat from the jacket, and the salt of the sea, believing that some of his soul was there in the fabric, his skin, his hair, his respiration and his heart; believing that if I concentrated hard enough, I might conjure him.

He had, in my mind and imagination, fused himself with my quest to bring Mam back, and with the vision of myself in the metallic dress storming the frozen, windy room.

"Oh, Mam," I whispered, closing my eyes and re-membering Francisco's heart beating against my neck. I thought I heard a change then in Mam's breathing, dry but active like the brush of wings, but as I pulled slightly back and looked at her, I realized it was my own breath-ing I'd heard.

Feeding Mam at the meal later, I was so far away in my thoughts of Francisco that I did not hear the words Da and Ishleen addressed to me until Da said, "It's hard enough that your mother cannot answer when we speak to her."

His words shocked me. I tried to stay focused, to keep myself present with Da and Ishleen and Old Peig. But all the things I did that were unrelated to Mam or the mem-ory of Francisco, I did with only half my heart.

The next day, a letter arrived from Donal and Fingal.

Dear Da, Maeve and Ishleen,

I felt a pulse of anger that they had not included Mam.

*There are good people in Ireland, always willing
to give a bed and food to a rebel. And if there
are no cottages on a hill or in a valley, there are
plenty of abandoned byres and bog holes. The
English are hated, and everyone we meet in every
village and on every boreen has a new story of
their atrocities. Suffice to say that we have a plan
and our rebellion is well organized, though we*

*cannot tell you more in a letter. We trust it will
reach you, but beware of treachery. Unfortunately,
as we know from our own Tom Cavan, its
potential exists in every small hamlet.*

*Your most faithful sons and brothers,
Donal and Fingal*

The next morning when Da, Ishleen and I set out to
fish, the waves were uneasy, cresting and whitening as
they moved toward land. I was facing the south waters in
the direction *La Hermana de la Luna* had gone when I
saw a slim dark boat appear out of a curtain of mist.
Standing straight up within was a woman in a gray-green
dress with long rivulets of wet hair clinging to her shoulders and arms, looking like someone who'd just come up
from the sea. I recognized her as the woman who had
lured Ishleen when Mrs. Cavan had taken me to Dungarven. My body went stiff and cold. I watched her every
tiny movement.

She focused on Ishleen, who, like my father, was looking in the direction of Woman's Crag.

As if propelled by some unnatural force, the woman's
craft brought her swiftly and silently closer, then stopped,
treading the waves about three yards away. Long leaves
of dark green kelp were interlaced with strands of her
hair, and some lay on her bodice in twists and curls like
ribbons. She bent slightly forward from the waist, her expression almost fierce, and showed me something metallic in her hand. I did not breathe. I could see that little

snails and pearls clung to the skin of her fingers and palm, but whatever she held reflected light so strongly that I could not discern what it was.

She stood up straight again and shivered on the air, so I thought she'd dissolve. Instead, she divided into three women, each a little different from the other, but all in wet dresses of gray-green. They came closer on their boat, which now looked more like half a giant unhinged seashell. I saw that the hems of their dresses were pulpy and a little transparent, and within the folds of that sleek, shiny fabric, I saw jellyfish, internal lights igniting on and off, causing eerie pale blue illuminations on the women's dresses. The vision became more and more uncanny: the water sloshed around the women's ankles; jellyfish writhed, convulsing gracefully, blossoming open and closed; and starfish walked the sides of the boat. What disturbed me more than anything else was the way two of the women were staring at Ishleen. The eyes of the one at the center, who was the original woman, kept flashing from me to Ishleen and back again to me.

Gradually the three women resolved back into one, and the boat shrank into a long dark craft not unlike my father's fishing boat. With a kind of sneer, the woman again held the metallic object up significantly, then tossed it into the water. She dissolved then, leaving the smell and charge of lightning on the air.

My father and Ishleen, who had not once turned around while this vision had taken place, remained oblivious, and I did not want to tell them about it.

That night after pulling in our catch, we were sorting through the fish when I found Francisco's compass among them. Its window was shattered, but the name *Las Santas Islas* and the triple spiral were still clearly visible.

Old Peig left when we arrived home, having been sent for by the family of a woman in childbirth. Though my mind was wildly distracted, I managed to prepare dinner but did not eat with Da and Mam and Ishleen. I lay down on my pallet facing the wall, stunned by the memory of the woman holding the shattered compass.

I took Francisco's jacket out from under the blanket and found that the silver cording on the shoulders issued light, mist rising from the fabric. And I feared, though I could hardly bear to consider it too closely, that Francisco might be dead. It seemed that the woman, or trinity of women, had been suggesting this to me.

I held the compass, but its solidity tormented me. Its hard, cold surfaces warmed under my breath and intensified the feeling of Francisco's absence. I placed the shattered compass in the front chest pocket of the jacket and pressed it to me. Each time my heart beat, I felt the compass needle quiver there, comforting me as if it were Francisco's heart beating against my own. From this, I tried to convince myself that I would see him again.

In my dream that night, the sea was crashing. Over the noise of the swells, I heard Francisco calling me. "Maeve! Maeve! Help me!"

I sat up, breathing fiercely. As quickly as I could, I put on my boots and went out, making my way in the moon-light to the overhang of the cave.

The water sloshed quietly in the dark. I went to the cave and found a candle we had left there. I brought it out, lit it and dripped hot wax onto the stone where the Spanish ghosts had been sitting the other night. Then I stuck the candle in place on the stone, the flame stirring and pulsing. Next to the candle I laid the jacket very carefully, then climbed to the threshold of the cave, the place where I had been standing when I'd first seen the dead Spaniards in their jackets. I resolved to wait as long as it might take for the two dead shipmates. I placed my hope in them, thinking they might be able to tell me where Francisco was. But now I realized with disap-pointment that the air did not feel the way it had that night.

The moon was only a smear behind the thick, smoky cloud cover, and the water had none of the clarity and brilliance from all the starlight. There was a vacancy now on the air, as if much of the vivacity from the time when Francisco had been here had departed with him.

Every slosh of tide at the rocks left an echo under the overhang.

I gazed back at the jacket. Even the issue of light from the silver cording was dull, and an awful sensation of emptiness swept over me.

Still, I wouldn't leave.

I remembered his promise to come back, and I was de-termined to wait for him.

Very early in the morning, just at the break of dawn, a fisherman passed in his boat and was startled by the sight of me: a wild thing on the rocks, my hair disheveled and blowing, grasping the coat of an armada Spaniard around my shoulders. The fisherman stood awkwardly in his craft and made the sign of the cross.

Da and Ishleen appeared on the rocks an hour or so later, calling me home. I was sitting on the stone shelf curled up into myself, not even caring that the tide was high and wetting me to the bone.

But with the sun up, there was little hope that Francisco might come. My heart had fallen so hard, I didn't want to move. I felt so helpless against what now felt like Mam's inevitable sinking away.

Da got his boat and steered it around to where I was.

"Come home now, Maeve," he said, and reached out to help me into the boat. When I looked into his eyes from under my wind-matted hair, I saw the same look he had given Mam when she'd heard the voice of the swan.

As we ascended the hill at Ard Macha, Da stopped to talk to a local man who told him about all the wreckage from Spanish ships in a confluence of rocks a few hours south of our shore.

After washing and dressing, and wearily sleeping away the afternoon, I heard Francisco's voice again calling me: "Maeve! Maeve! Help me!"

I prepared for another night's vigil among the rocks. It was as if I couldn't help myself.

This time I did not remain in the rocks near the caves, but walked south along the shore in the direction the ship had gone. Some of the wreckage I saw was from Francisco's original ship. I knew, because I found a warped broken board with the blistered decomposing letters of the word *Soledad* on it. But, finding no signs of *La Hermana de la Luna*, I tripped my way back toward Ard Macha, the wick of my lamp now dark and quenched in oil.

It was dawn when I saw Da and Ishleen appear in the boat, with despondent expressions. Shivering, I got in with them.

Ishleen looked wistful.

"I think Francisco is in trouble, Ishleen. I hear him calling me."

Her eyes darkened, but she said nothing.

Da pulled the boat up onto the sand, and I got out, but Ishleen stayed with him to go out fishing that day.

In Da's search to find me, other residents had come out to lend a hand. When they saw that I was safe, most of them disbanded, but as I climbed the hill back to the cottage, Mrs. Molloy and Mrs. Callahan were standing there. They stared as I carried the burned-out lamp, my hems torn and soaked, my hair matted from the wind.

"She's like her own mother, as mad as the mist and snow," one of them said.

Tears streaked my face as I heard this, but I was not dissuaded.

"Look at her, wearing the coat of a dead Spaniard," the other whispered.

When I was inside the cottage, I laid Francisco's jacket on a chair near the fire, to dry from the mist and salt spray. My skin was hot and feverish, and my stomach felt queasy. I knelt before Mam, who was in her wheeled chair facing the fire, hanging her head. Her eyes were three quarters of the way closed, inward-looking. Her breathing was very faint. I laid my head in her lap and cried.

That night before the meal, Da took me aside and told me that he had to leave early the next morning for Killybegs. The remaining men of the Ard Macha faction were going to meet to discuss more action against the English and to try to find a way to bring aid to the fugitives.

"You can't keep traipsing off every night this way, Maeve," he said. "You've got to stay here and take care of Ishleen and your mam."

Nervous at the danger he faced and the gravity of the situation, I promised him I'd not do it again. And even though I heard Francisco's voice, I didn't go out for three nights.

But on the fourth night that Da was gone, I felt an intense expectation on the air, a certainty that Francisco was waiting for me. The moon was large and hung in a clear sky. I told myself I'd go down to the overhang while Ishleen was asleep but come back well before dawn, and she'd never know that I'd gone. As I was planning this out in my thoughts, she awoke, having somehow sensed what was on my mind.

"There is a storm ring around the moon," she said softly as we stood by the open door, looking out. She peered into my distracted face. "There will be wind and very high tides in the morning."

I had not noticed until she'd pointed it out, but she was right. A slender aura of luminous fog encircled the moon, the promise of tumultuous weather.

"If you go," she said, "something bad will happen."

"I'm not going anywhere, Ishleen."

But even after I tucked her into bed and kissed her on the temple, she looked uneasily at me.

CHAPTER 14

Deep in the night, when I went outside, the sky was lit up with the moon and portending storm, flashes of trembling light breaking between massive clouds. I got into the boat and sailed away from the land. A violent wind blew me miles to the south until I beached on a rocky isle, where I came upon a dozen bodies of dead Spaniards lying facedown in the sand. All were wearing the purple jackets, the mysterious white steam rising from the silver cording and disappearing on the air. The tide had soaked them all through, and ran in again now, flooding them and retreating in jetties of foam.

With great effort, I turned each man onto his back and bent over him, searching for signs of life. I wiped sand from their faces, pushed and cajoled until I knew with certainty that each was dead. I was sweating, in spite of the blistering wind and icy salt sparks from the tides. My heart pumped hard, my eyes raking the shore for any others.

It was then that I saw the torn side of a hull, bobbing and stuck between rocks. Words were painted there but partially obscured with kelp. I waded in up to my thighs to where the rocks were high, jagged and numerous. Their black surfaces were slippery; it was with effort that I managed to climb them and come close enough to move the kelp and read the words: *La Hermana de la Luna*.

Turning, I saw the figurehead from the ship, the one that Francisco had insisted looked like me. It was presiding over something in a pool between three or four large peaked stones, something I thought at first was a sea plant, dark fringes waving in unison with the sloshing water. As I pulled myself along toward it, the figurehead's eyes flashed to mine, peering at me for a few moments before looking down again at whatever she was watching over. As I got closer, my perspective grew clearer and I saw that it was the hair of someone in the water.

When I reached the edge of the rock, I could see the poor soul quite clearly. It was the sailor who had come out in the little boat to bring Francisco back to the ship, the one who had told me that Francisco promised to come back for me. Only his head was above the water-line, leaning back against the rock. His eyes were open, staring but unseeing. His arms were rising slightly from his sides in the water, and softly bobbing on the cold current. I leaned far over the stone, desperate to bring him up somehow, when I saw that one of his legs was caught under a piece of fallen wreckage. It held him there, suspended underwater.

I pushed on the various stones that surrounded him, to see which might be movable, and found that one of them rocked and might be shifted. With my entire body, I pushed until I got it out of the way and, swimming down, pulled the wreckage away from his feet. Despite my exhaustion, I began to drag him ashore; at one point, still half in the water, I stopped to rest, pressing his body near a rock wall. I felt how intensely cold he was. Though it made little sense to do so, I wriggled out of the deluged jacket I wore and wrapped the sailor in it.

Then, as I continued to try to drag him to shore, a strong tide came in. I lost hold of his body, and it went seaward, then under a wave. I swam down after it. The moon shone in a long beam of light into the water, illuminating him, his arms raised all the way up now, as he stared ahead unseeing. I caught him, struggling hard to bring him up by swimming with one arm and holding him with the other, but the effort was too great and he slipped from me, continuing to plummet.

Panicked, I pulled myself deeper, swimming after him, when my need to breathe grew desperate. I had to rush upward and break the surface, gasping for air.

When I went down again, my hopes of helping the Spaniard faded. He was nowhere to be seen. I resurfaced to breathe, but decided to try once more. My heart jumped with hope as I saw a shadow coming up from a great depth. But as it ascended, I realized that it was the jacket floating there, open-armed and filled with water. Remembering what Francisco had said about keeping him alive, I swam down after it, but the waves had become choppy. The forceful push and pull of the water played havoc with me. I thought I was finally getting close, when the water pulled me suddenly away from the jacket.

A figure that seemed to be wearing a dark gray cape appeared in the depths and came swimming quickly toward me, revealing itself to be a kind of stingray, a wide flat kite-shaped creature with human hands and an angry human face. It bared its jagged teeth and planted a bite on my shoulder, sharp and painful. I screamed, the sound muted by the water.

Four women similar in visage to the Swan Woman approached us in a frenzied swim, driving the creature off. As I swam to the surface, aching to breathe, the women also rose upward, turning into swans as they reached the air. Each ascended to the sky with a tremendous shriek as the light of dawn began to break. Three of them flew westward, while the other hovered close above a few yards away, as if to show me Da's little boat, which was bobbing on a wave below it.

My shoulder ached badly and bled, and my arms were intensely tired as I trod water and made my way toward the boat. When I got in, the swan flew over me as if magically propelling the boat back north. The dawn light had now driven off the shadows of night. I had not intended to be so long away, and found myself anxious to be home, praying that Ishleen had not awakened and found me gone.

I was almost back at Ard Macha when, to my shock, I saw a small boat riding seaward from the shore, rocking unsteadily. Recognizing Tom Cavan in the bow, rowing the craft, I felt an intimation of dread. A woman in gray-green sat in the boat, too, hunched forward and holding something contained in glass. Neither seemed to see me in the periphery. With tremendous effort, I rowed forward, struggling to see what the woman was holding. It was small, too insubstantial to be called a figure, yet it had a shimmer and a form, and moved within the glass that contained it. For flashes of moments, it took on a solidity. Straining to see, I recognized it suddenly as the transparent figure of a child. Just as my heart sped with suspicion, the swan flew toward them and began screeching.

The little transparent figure grew opaque as it looked up at the swan, and in that instant I recognized a ghostly Ishleen. I cried out, but my voice was drowned by the violent rush and crash of the sea. Soon the boat was swallowed by a sudden mist that opened like a curtain, revealing something massive floating there, a flash of ice and light, before it was again obscured.

I tried to row after them, but a powerful surge lifted my craft from below. The clouds rent apart, and rain fell in a deluge. The sea carried the boat to the shore against my will, lodging it between stones on the high beach. I ran up to the cottage and found Old Peig inside, sitting forward on a chair as if stunned.

"Peig!" I cried.

She turned her head slowly and looked at me, her eyes wet with tears. She hesitated, then lifted a trembling arm and pointed to the yellow curtain, which was pulled closed. I went and drew it open.

Ishleen lay limply beside Mam, wearing the same vacant expression Mam wore. I sat on the edge of the bed and touched her arm.

"Ishleen! Ishleen!" I whispered, shaking her gently.

"She won't wake," Old Peig said. "She came to me before dawn when she found you gone. I came back here with her to wait for you. She was playing outside just as dawn was breaking. The door was open and I could hear her singing to herself the way she does. But then she was quiet, and when I said her name, she didn't answer. I went out and found her sitting on the ground. I said her name and she didn't turn. As I went toward her, I saw Tom Cavan and a strange woman rushing into a boat. I think they've carried off her spirit the way they did with your mam."

"Do you think they have Mam, too?" I asked.

"It's the same awful devilry at work here," she said, and pointed to Ishleen. "I think they must."

"What do I do, Peig?" I pleaded.

She shook her head.

I ran outside, but the water was still too unsteady and the wind too high for me to attempt going after them. Clouds bulged with seemingly endless rain. I heard on the air itself the voice of the swan, which I could no longer see. It had now flown into the distance, leaving a vague, melancholy echo.

That night I lay with Mam and Ishleen on the box bed, leaning my face close to my sister's, making sure of her steady, transparent breathing. Exhaustion set in and I closed my eyes.

The light was very blue, like late dusk or early dawn. A quiet wind was blowing and the sea was still. I was staring at the ruins when I saw an opening through the tower, a dark doorway with faint illumination like candlelight within. I went in and descended a staircase. The place was rough, dilapidated walls and crumbling passageways. I heard Ishleen's soft breathing and followed the sound into a once-elegant room with a great canopied bed, now collapsed; the walls and furniture were dusty and decrepit.

Everywhere I looked, I saw the triple spiral carved into furniture in decorative repeated patterns, embroidered on the faded bed curtains. On the wall was a framed portrait of a little girl. I approached and recognized it as Ishleen, but she was feathered along the hairline like the mysterious woman who had given me the bottles for protection, and was wearing a cloak of white feathers, and a crown. Below the portrait was a mirror, shattered and etched with cracks, flecked black in places, so my own reflection was unclear. A piece of the mirror, big enough to fit into the palm of my hand, broke off and fell to my feet.

"Take it," I heard a disembodied female voice urge. "You will need this when you go."

"When I go where?" I asked, looking around me for the source of the voice.

But there was no answer.

I looked again at the portrait of Ishleen, but it had transformed into a portrait of a swan.

I awakened, and sat up panting and disoriented. Mam and Ishleen lay in the same vacant postures they had been in when I had fallen asleep. In my hand was the jagged piece of mirror. Shocked, I tried to understand how this could have occurred. My heart beat swiftly, and I listened for the weather. The wind had gone silent. I dressed and put the compass and the piece of mirror into my pocket.

Outside, streamers of sunlight threshed through the clouds. The sea was calm and could be, I decided, easily navigated. I went down and dislodged Da's boat from the rocks. When I turned around, I gasped, wondering if I was still dreaming.

The Swan Woman was there, looking expectantly at me, her garment so white that it glowed in the sunlight. Her shoulders, I noticed, were taut, as if they might transform at a moment's notice into wings.

"Maeve," she said to me urgently, leaning slightly forward from the waist. "You cannot approach that ice barge alone and unprotected."

"Are they there through that mist? My sister and mother?" I asked.

"Yes."

"Has my mother been there all this time?"

She nodded. "Though the ice barge has not always been at anchor this close to Ard Macha."

I was flooded with anxiety. "All this time, she's been on that barge waiting for someone to help her. I've got to go there and get them both back!"

I showed her the compass and the mirror, and told her how I had come upon each.

"The creature who lives on that barge was a battle goddess. Her name is Uria," she explained. "The women in gray-green are some of her henchwomen. They taunted you with the compass, believing it was powerless because it was shattered. Instead, they provided you with an invaluable tool. For you, the needle is still sensitive and alive. You will need these items, but neither is enough to protect you. You will be killed if you try to approach."

"What can I do? How can I save my sister and my mother?"

"I will tell you how you should go there, but first I have to tell you what you must do."

Clouds were now gathering above us, their shadows moving across the landscape. Her eyes darted around uneasily.

"Somewhere on Uria's barge, there is a jewel the size of a small apple, very cold to the touch but with a look of bright fire about it. It is called the Fire Opal. You must do everything you can to find it."

"Why?" I asked. "What is its power?"

"I can't tell you this, but you must find it, and when you do, guard it with your life. Danu needs it."

"But what about my mother and sister?" I asked.

"I can only tell you that we are at the very precipice of a new cycle in nature. In order to save your mother and sister, you must first do this."

As the moments passed, the feathers she wore looked more and more like they were growing directly from her skin rather than sewn to the fabric of her cloak.

Each time I had seen this woman, she had been in a different stage of transformation from swan into woman, or woman into swan.

"Tom Cavan's unearthing of the armor five years ago, the day the first Ishleen fell ill and died, brought Uria back into the waters just beyond this shore. Uria, too, is after something she lost, without which she is incapacitated. She has made Tom Cavan her assistant, and he has been helping her search all these years for it. Tom has become indispensable to her. She liked that he killed birds for sport and encouraged him to continue doing it, fearing that Danu's children might return to Ireland in bird form."

"Why don't the two goddesses meet and resolve what's between them?"

"Uria can never penetrate Danu's exile. Only the very subtle can survive the journey through the Realm of the Shee, which leads to Danu's Holy Isles. Besides, Uria knows that what she is missing is somewhere in Ireland, and most likely in Ard Macha, where it was lost to her seven centuries ago. But she cannot walk land without it, and thus Tom Cavan has become her agent."

"What is it that Uria's lost?"

"I don't know all the answers, and besides, I can't take the time," she said, her eyes darting toward the bog or up to the hill. She seemed to mistrust the very atmosphere of Ard Macha.

"During his long absences, Tom Cavan lives splendidly on Uria's barge," she went on. "He has been watching everything here for her, and it was he who orchestrated the abduction of Ishleen. He recognized that the bottle she wore around her neck kept her safe, and he tricked her somehow into removing it."

"That devil!" I muttered.

"What you must do, you will see, will go against every emotion you feel for Tom Cavan."

"What?" I asked.

"Go to his mother's house and tell her that you want to accept his proposal of marriage."

I stared at her as if she had slapped me.

"She will take you to him on Uria's barge. It is too carefully guarded by abysmal creatures for you to go there alone to try to save your mother and sister. You must go to Mrs. Cavan as if in despair.

"There is a kind of ventilation system to the ice barge, air shafts that connect every room and corridor, prevent-.ing the ice from fully closing off. When you find the Fire Opal, which is what you must do, eat this leaf, then light this pastille and put it into the main air current. The smoke is narcotic and very swiftly moving. It will inundate the air of the barge. Everyone will fall asleep, but the leaf will keep it from affecting you. Take the Fire Opal downstairs to the lowest level and get into one of the small boats. Let your compass lead you to Danu's isle.

"You have only three days to return before they all awaken. You must be expedient, or the ghost souls of your mother and sister will be in danger."

Some sound or shift in the light startled her. In a flurry she transformed into a swan and rose into the sky with a melancholy shriek.

Overwhelmed by thoughts of what might be ahead of me, I remained where I was, watching her and listening to the brush of her wings as she flew seaward.

Part Three

The Ice Barge

CHAPTER 15

I t seemed a long time before Mrs. Cavan came to the door once I'd knocked. When she did, she opened it only a crack and peered out at me with one wide-open eye.

"May I speak with you, Mrs. Cavan?" I asked.

She hesitated, a wrinkle deepening over her brow, before she allowed me in.

I was astonished. This was not the cottage I remembered at all: big upholstered pieces of furniture; sweeps of fine curtains over the windowless walls; velvet and silk brocades; exquisite things, as if she had bought out the entire Muldoon's shop. Even the kettle was solid gold, and lined up on the mantel were crystal goblets and fine china cups with their saucers leaning upright behind them.

There was no sign of the old furnishings: the rush-and-cane chairs, the rough wood table, the mattress stuffed with hay. And unless they were in the shadow behind one of the brocade curtains, the sow and her sucklings were nowhere to be seen.

Mrs. Cavan herself was festooned, almost outrageously so, in feathers and lace.

Yet there was something eerie about the light in the house, an atmosphere of shadows and pale iridescent glitter. The light seemed to be missing some important quality that light needed. The entire effect was unsettling and caused a slight pounding in my temples. I tried to figure out what was wrong with this illumination, and what its source might be.

In my peripheral vision, the curtains and furniture seemed to be shivering, but when I looked directly at anything, it took on solidity. I reached across to the surface of a gold and green silk curtain, and when my fingertips grazed it, a very faint smoke or steam appeared.

I turned around and found Mrs. Cavan peering up at me intently.

"Are you expecting company?" I asked, focusing on her clothes.

"No, Maeve. Since Tom has come into a small fortune, I dress this way every day and for my own pleasure."

"And what of Mr. Cavan?" I asked. "Has he not come back from English custody?"

One side of her mouth twitched at the question.

"No," she said curtly. "Why are you here?"

Her harsh gaze belied a hushed expectancy. It was all I

could do to remain calm. "I have decided to accept Tom's proposal," I answered. "It is, as he said, inevitable that we marry."

Her eyes widened. She let out a strange extended sigh and said in a small voice, "He will be very gratified." She focused hard on me again. "I always knew things would turn out the way he wanted. I'm going to take you to him."

"Where is he?"

Little fireworks went off in her eyes. "He's on a beautiful ship, more like a kingdom on the waves. Everything you could want is there." She grew thoughtful, then looked at me from under her brows. "No one trusted me when I expounded on his qualities. You didn't."

I tensed but forced myself to respond. "I understand now."

She searched my eyes a little nervously, but whether she trusted me or not, she was excited to bring me to Tom and began to fuss about the room in preparation.

She took a lit lamp from a sconce on the wall and, sweeping aside a purple velvet curtain, beckoned me to follow her through a door in the hard, rough limestone wall.

"Come," she said, gesticulating with excitement. When I crossed the threshold, I found myself at the top of a steep staircase that had been dug and carved directly inside the hill of Ard Macha. As she descended, Mrs. Cavan's swinging lamp illuminated fossilized seashells and delicate spiders, trembling and glistening as they crept over the cavelike walls.

After a dizzying descent, the staircase became a passageway, and the farther we went, the more I could smell the saline proximity of the ocean. Suddenly we reached a slender ascending staircase carved of stone that ended at a doorway. It opened onto a jutting rock crag, the ocean splashing about five feet below. What I saw as I stood there stunned me.

About thirty feet away, a massive drift of ice, partially carved to look like a ship, exuded a shimmering solitude, anxious seabirds mewing and screeching in the air around it. Half of it was rough and unformed, while the other half was beautifully detailed as if by fine artisans, with frozen towers and pinnacles and terraces. The entire thing was encased in its own wide dome of mist.

Numerous transparent carvings of faces and figures lined the upper tiers of ice, lit from within with shivering bright lights, some pale gold, some white. I was startled to perceive tiny figures—little girls, I realized as I squinted—hanging suspended on rope swings, busily carving and chipping at the ice, forming delicate embellishments around arched windows at the towers.

The entire structure emitted a subtle steam, the sea splashing at it, waves refracting on the ice walls.

At the lowest tier of the barge, closest to the water, the ice was carved into lanes or piers where a few small boats were docked.

A whistle sounded, and out of one of those lanes a small boat with no one in it came toward us through the waves, moving forward purposefully, as if navigated by some invisible being. We stepped into it, and it turned, taking us back to the barge, the low roar of the swells beneath us.

We docked, then climbed out of the boat onto the ice pier, went up a staircase that rose directly out of the water, and walked through an arch to a landing, still not too far above the water level. It was a wet open-air entranceway crowded with hordes of disfigured mermaids similar to the one who had bitten me.

"They're guards," Mrs. Cavan said. "They usually swim around the ice but are waiting out a tidal shift."

The sea splashed up and in, wetting our shoes and hems and rolling over the thick supine bodies of the mermaids, then slapped the walls as it exited.

One of the creatures—I was certain it was the one who had tried to pull Mam into the undertow when she was pregnant—hoisted herself up to look at me. Her large blue-scaled tail pointed tensely up and abruptly slapped down hard against the ice. She screamed as she focused on me, and many of the others grew agitated. They were all unhappy-looking with distressed faces. The one who knew me bared her jagged teeth as she peered at me, and began to foam at the mouth.

"She's with me!" Mrs. Cavan shouted at them. "She's going to marry Tom."

This news seemed to unsettle some of them, and they slapped their tails hard against the ice floor, screamed and made agonized, inarticulate noises. *They* couldn't also be enamored of Tom Cavan, I thought, horrified.

"Such dangerous creatures," I commented, half under my breath.

"In the sea they are terrors, but on land or on the ice like this, they are much less frightening than Uria's other protectors," Mrs. Cavan said. "Besides, they're only a threat if you are a traitor to Uria, or . . . ." She turned and looked at me as if her mistrust for me pierced her again. "If you prove to be devious in one way or another."

As we climbed up to the next landing, I became aware of an amplified breathing and the sound of a heart beating, as if the ice barge itself were alive.

"What is that?" I asked, looking around for the source.

"That's Uria, the goddess. Her breathing and heartbeat can be heard throughout this floating palace. Tom says that her nervous system is the central pulse of this entire barge."

Once we were at the next level, my heart raced as I recognized the vast, drafty ballroom, empty of any furnishings, its floor of polished ice reflecting everything above it with the clarity of a mirror. I was certain it was the place I had always seen in my vision. Everything had a dull blue cast to it, duller even than the unsettling lack of color in Mrs. Cavan's cottage. Here, though the overall impression of the light was blue, it felt drained of life, not pleasant like most blues. The walls, carved of ice, were encrusted in places with frost, and the gusting wind glimmered with particles.

The massive chandelier, hanging with icicles, swayed

and chimed above us as a cold wind moved through the room and out into the corridors. Just as in my vision, there was a vast emptiness about the room, in spite of elaborate white and pale blue decorative plasterwork on the walls.

Then I saw the door to the other room, the room I was sure Mam was in. I steadied myself and continued to follow Mrs. Cavan obediently. Every step through the corridors echoed loudly beneath our feet, setting off a series of echoes, which, however loud, never eclipsed the pervasive breathing and heartbeat of Uria.

"It sounds as if the goddess is sleeping now," Mrs. Cavan commented to me over her shoulder. "We must be moving through her dream."

She turned suddenly and stopped. "I should explain," she said. "You won't actually meet Uria. She stays isolated in one area, her own wing off the farthest corridor, and no one is allowed to go there.

"She does have an emanation, a figure that represents her, and you will probably meet that emanation tomorrow night. But not even Tom has been in the presence of the actual goddess." She leaned her face close to mine, and her eyes bulged with emphasis as she said, "And *he* is the most important person in her palace."

With a self-satisfied and gloating expression, she looked almost accusingly at me, then whipped her head back around and continued on her way.

In one very long room that we passed but did not enter, I saw what looked like dead bodies behind a thin layer of ice on the wall, some frozen in the act of twisting or struggling, others slumping forward as if surrendering to a dark fate.

I wanted to stop, go inside, and look closer at this awful scene, but Mrs. Cavan rushed me through. "Tom is likely in the dining hall at this hour," she said.

A harsh gust of wind blew and moaned as we approached a set of massive doors. Dread seized me as Mrs. Cavan turned the knob and it made a loud, squeaking noise.

Inside, her son was slumped over a long table big enough for fifty people, his head on his plate, a wine goblet spilled over beside him. The ruffled cuffs of his sky-blue velvet jacket, drained of its vibrant color in this light, were stained with wine.

Another man sat at the opposite end of the table, also in a drunken stupor, facedown, arms outstretched. He was wearing the uniform of an English soldier. Three more English soldiers lay passed out on the floor.

"It's too late!" Mrs. Cavan cried. "He's had his dinner."

She gestured for me to step out, then closed the door with a boom and lead me up a new corridor.

"Why was he with English soldiers?"

She gave me a frown and a dismissive wave of the hand.

She opened a creaking door to another room. We entered, and I was stunned to see my missing dress, the one I'd labored so hard over, on a dressmaker's dummy, the hem rippling, the sleeves lifting and flapping in the gusting winds. Next to it stood another dressmaker's form, this one bare but fitted, I thought, to the measurements of my body, and beside it, bolts of heavy silvery or metallic fabric.

"My missing dress!" I shot Mrs. Cavan a suspicious look, at which she stiffened and recoiled.

"You seem ungrateful. You ought to consider yourself lucky that I have anticipated this turn of events."

I looked at her cautiously.

"You've been ungrateful to me in the past, Maeve," she said, and I knew she was referring to the time I'd rejected the gift at the Dungarven shop.

At that moment, I saw movement. Sitting on the floor, studying the stitch work on the hem of the dress, was a young girl, perhaps fifteen years old, wearing a colorful fur-lined hat. Her skin was very pale blue, and she had about her a gaunt, skeletal grace. Gazing at me with large eyes both brimming and deep, she held mine a beat longer than she might have, so I sensed in her a desire to talk with me.

"I am having dresses made for you, Maeve," Mrs. Cavan said. Then she turned to the girl. "There are specifications," she said to the girl, then bent over and whispered into her ear. A shadow passed over the girl's brow, as if she did not like what she was hearing.

The girl's eyes flashed meaningfully in my direction. I recognized a plea in her expression.

I heard a blast echoing through the room, a crash, and a sound of groaning.

"It is only the ice outside," the girl said, noticing my

169

unease. "It breaks and shifts. It sounds like it's in pain, doesn't it?"

"Yes," I said.

Mrs. Cavan took me to a nearby room where I would sleep. Like all the other rooms I'd seen so far, it was vast and echoing, the few pieces of furniture all elegant and crowded into one area. The bed had a canopy and curtains, and there were carved white plasterwork figures and faces on the walls, most of them frosted over with ice.

Mrs. Cavan gave me a nightdress, then lit the fire in the grate.

"Let me offer you a little advice, Maeve," she said. "Be grateful and don't ask a lot of questions."

It seemed to me that Uria had paused in her breathing to listen to Mrs. Cavan's words, but I wasn't sure.

With the lights out, the firelight around the coals was a deeper blue than any color I'd seen here so far. Never having seen blue fire, I was fascinated and got near it, hoping to warm myself against the frigid air, but it did not seem to issue any warmth at all.

There was one carved face among all the others that had no ice on it, and that was on the mantel just above the grate of the fireplace. It wore an odd expression, its teeth set together, so I could not tell if a sudden soft hissing noise I heard was coming from the face or the fire itself.

*　*　*

There was no possible way I could sleep. The thought that Mam's and Ishleen's ghosts were trapped here some-where drove me to leave the bed in a cold ecstasy.

A candle with a blue flame was burning just outside my room, so I took it with me, advancing into the dark corridors, listening carefully all the time to the amplified breathing and steady drumbeats of Uria's heart, trying to remember from my vision the way back to the ballroom.

I pushed a door, and as it emitted a ghostly twang, my candle flared as if in a draft, and I found myself in the long room where the mass of struggling figures ran a great length of the ice wall. I held the flame up to the faces. None belonged to anyone I had ever known.

I heard voices whispering in Spanish, the names of ships: *Santa Maria de la Luz, Nuestra Señora de la Soledad, Santa Rita.* These were, every one of them, ar-mada Spaniards, all their bodies held hostage in a long row in the ice. Suddenly I heard one whisper *"La Her-mana de la Luna."* I stopped cold, recognizing a face: one of Francisco's shipmates from *La Hermana de la Luna,* the one who had waved from the galleon after Francisco had boarded. I gasped, and my candle pulsed before his face, grotesquely lit from below. I had not seen this man on the beach among the other dead, and now I wondered if Francisco was also here.

I searched every face but did not find him.

I thought of the illuminated carved ice figures on the upper terraces of the barge, and found a staircase that ran outside in open air and up to the outer decks. There were hundreds, maybe thousands, of carvings, not like the

Spaniards with real bodies behind ice, but hollow ice carvings filled with pale illumination, some trembling or pulsing, some bright, some dim, and it looked as if they were all female images. It was both breathtaking and deeply disturbing, the lit ice and the suggestion of grace-ful faces and figures.

There were so many, and a raging wind blew gusts so frigid that my head ached as I stood there. How strange: this barge was close to Ard Macha, yet it felt arctic, colder than any place I'd ever been.

I heard a creak and turned.

A tiny figure of a girl wearing the same multicolored hat that the seamstress had worn, a few soft tufts of hair peeking out from under it, stood ill clad, shivering and barefoot at the head of the stairs I had just ascended. I stared at her, then turned again when a shadow moved above me on the air. A massive vulture was circling around, then came down and landed, its heavy talons clutching at a rail. It perched itself only six or seven feet away from me. Extending its wings, stretching them to their full span, it underwent an eerie transformation: its head, neck and chest became human and female, while the rest of it remained a vulture. My heart sped. The creature's head came suddenly forward, and she nar-rowed her amber eyes at me, then smiled, showing her teeth. Terror tingled at the tip of my every nerve.

When I looked again, the little girl had disappeared, but I could hear her soft footfalls growing distant.

I ran back toward the stairs I had come up and began to descend. As I rushed through the echoing chambers, an arctic blast followed me. I found myself moving through the vast room of my vision, the chandelier swinging with great agitation and twanging melodiously. I noted with tremendous relief that Uria's breathing and heartbeat remained calm and steady, and I hoped that meant that she was oblivious of my trespassing.

I felt a twinge of panic when I sensed someone watching me. Looking to my left, I saw the door to the mysterious room slightly ajar and the tiny figure of the girl peering out, beckoning me inside.

CHAPTER 16

Still flustered, the cautious side of me ached to find my way back to my room and hide under the covers, but there was such urgency in the way the girl had gestured to me, and such a pulsating and fateful sensation associated with that door, that I rushed toward her.

The room we entered was a dim and bitterly cold space glimmering with blue candlelight and crowded with ice sculptures. Little girls, all wearing the signature colorful winter hat and a similar thick fur-lined dress, stood before one sculpture or another, gazing at it or whispering quietly, as if they were praying in a chapel. The seamstress who had made eye contact with me earlier turned from the ice figure she stood before and looked at us, then opened her arms to the tiny creature who had lured me there. The little one rushed into the embrace and let herself be warmed.

"I'm Gudrun," the older girl said quietly as she approached me. "This is Phee. She does not speak, but she *sees.*"

I looked at her questioningly.

"Intuition and premonitions," Gudrun explained.

In little Phee's haunted eyes, I saw a disarming combination of childlike wistfulness and dark human wisdom. Her clothes were more worn and faded than the clothes of the others, sewn and patched in places, and tattered.

I looked around the room. "This is my mother," Gudrun said, nodding toward the ice sculpture she had just been looking at.

Quite distinct from the bodies of the Spaniards in the ice, these were very much the same as the sculptures I'd seen on deck, clear and delicately carved, as if made of glass, and containing pulsations of light.

"These contain the ghost souls of our mothers," Gudrun said, gesturing at the many ice figures around the chapel.

Other girls in the colorful hats stood before other frozen womanly sculptures, looking at them yearningly, or bent before them lost in thought.

Phee touched my shoulder and pointed to two ice figures: one tall and a much shorter one, sequestered in an icy shadow in a far corner of the room.

My heart began to race. At my approach, I heard

voices, soft and vibrating, but so diffused that they were impossible to understand.

"Do you hear? Listen closely. These are the voices of your mother and sister in the ice," Gudrun said.

The renderings of Mam and little Ishleen, wearing placid, resigned expressions, were each clearly recognizable, and their blurred voices caused my heart to swell painfully.

"I carved the ice for them," said a familiar-looking little girl about twelve years old. I realized she had been one of the girls chiseling decorations on the ice barge when I'd arrived. She was introduced as Wheeta.

"You can hear their voices, but sadly, you cannot quite understand what they are saying. And you cannot embrace them," Wheeta warned, "because the heat of your body will cause the sculpture to melt a little, and they'd lose their contours. There must remain a gulf of cold between you."

"Mam! Ishleen!" I kept uttering, looking up at them on the ice slab where their sculptures were set, clouds of condensation from my breath on the air between us.

"We are the tundra girls," Gudrun said. "Uria long ago extracted the ghost souls from our mothers' bodies but keeps them here so that we will continue to work for her.

"Phee recognized you immediately, although I have to admit, I too felt that you were not one of those others. Not like Mrs. Cavan and her son. Especially after Mrs. Cavan gave me the dress you made. It still retains a very faint oil from your soul on it."

"Oil?" I asked.

"Anything we create with all of our selves is lubricated a little bit by our souls."

I realized that my teeth were chattering, and I was shaking so hard that I couldn't stand still. "It *is* freezing in here," Gudrun said. "Yet some girls sleep curled at the feet of their frozen mothers. Some girls die from the cold. There have been casualties among us."

"Why do they do this to you?" I asked, my heart heavy.

"There are some things we understand about our predicament, and some things we don't. We are from a lost tribe of Danu's children, displaced nomads who used to move slowly across the realms of cold. We were a shape-shifting society, as all of Danu's children were, but we were specifically half blue narwhal, the horned whale. Our fathers and brothers swam the shores parallel to the paths our women and daughters traveled on land. It was us, the females, who carved caves out of the ice with spades and torches of fire. Often we moved through sunless lands where it was always night and bitter cold. We are creative by nature, as you can see. Many women and girls carved embellishments in the ice, and even carved towers and gargoyles. Impermanence was our way of life. We'd leave our fanciful architecture behind us, and of course, the elements most likely erased much of it, though we have heard that there are places where these carvings are still pristine, and we dream of one day seeing them again and remembering ourselves as we were long ago in a happier time."

Gudrun's words prompted me to gaze up at Mam and Ishleen, and the illumination behind the ice brightened and glowed. I, too, longed for those happier times.

Gudrun resumed. "At night, our fathers and brothers came ashore with their catch and transformed into their human skins. It was at dusk, while waiting for our fathers and brothers after lighting our torches, that we used to stand on the cliffs and sing 'The Canticle of Fire.' That is how Uria first came across us, having heard us from her floating iceberg almost seven centuries ago, not long after her terrible battle with Danu. One of her vulture women in human form came to us and commissioned our mothers, who were true geniuses, to carve Uria's iceberg into a floating palace. Five of our mothers were priest-esses with druid knowledge. Not only did Uria want all the walls embellished, fit for a sovereign, but she wanted our mothers to use their understanding of the acoustics of the ice and enable her to hear everything that was said in every room on this 'palace.'

"There were two rules Uria had: no true fire could be brought aboard the barge—only the blue fire could pro-vide light and the illusion of warmth; and her own corri-dor, the one in which she lived, was off-limits.

"In the evenings, after working to carve her palace all day, we would return to the shore to meet our fathers and brothers. We would light our torches outside our own ice caves and sing 'The Canticle of Fire.' Uria's emanation would stand rapt on the deck listening. That song has power for Uria, the song that honors the element of fire, which is forbidden here. Uria's emanation used to watch the distant burning fires as if she coveted them. She still makes us sing 'The Canticle of Fire' once a week at least, these past seven centuries. Ice seems to be her element and her safety, yet in some way, she romanticizes fire."

"Imagine!" Wheeta uttered wistfully, staring off into the blue candlelight along one wall of the chapel. "Isn't it curious?"

"Every morning when our fathers and brothers transformed and took to the sea," Gudrun went on, "we traveled by small boat back to this barge to work. It was unusual that our mothers had accepted this commission, but we realized that they had some kind of plan. They understood something about Uria that they had not told us. We did not know that they recognized the evil here. Against Uria's orders, they left deaf spots, places they could speak to one another where Uria would not be able to hear them. We did not know that one of their plans all along was to build a system into this barge in which true fire would infiltrate and melt the ice that preserved the goddess. Their plans, we would later realize, were dangerous, and that is why we were not privy to them.

"But one day while all of us girls were carving on the outside, a group of Uria's vulture women asked us very politely to come inside. It was to this very room we came. We were each presented with a block of ice and encouraged to carve statues of our mothers, a task we each engaged in happily. At the end of the day, our mothers did not come, but the vulture women led us to a room where we were fed. The door was locked behind us, and we spent a miserable uncertain night, unable to rest, waiting anxiously for our mothers to appear. The next day we were led back to this room. All of our mothers' statues contained tremulous light, and we heard a riot of indiscernible words, but all of us recognized the pitch and treble of our mothers' voices. Their ghost souls had been extricated from their bodies and trapped in the ice. The five priestesses among our mothers, it turned out, had trespassed into Uria's quarters, and had also brought true fire onto the ship, trying to create a forge oven in the basement. The vulture women managed to get rid of the true fire, and Uria enslaved us."

Gudrun came close to me, the blue flames glowing in her large eyes. She spoke quietly then and with great sadness. "We do not grow here. We are girls eternally, longing for our mothers. And because it is our nature to be deeply attached to them, we remain here, tending to their vacant bodies and devoting ourselves to their ghost souls preserved in the ice. We learned later that a vast net had been spread and our fathers and brothers, who had approached the barge to find us, had been trapped, and most of them probably died. If any of them survived, it is likely that they intermarried with non-shape-shifting narwhals, and over the centuries forgot their shape-shifting ancestry, as you have likely forgotten your own.

"For all these centuries, that basement where the tundra priestesses were trying to build the forge for true fire has been closed off from the rest of the barge. The five daughters of the five priestess mothers who designed the system live isolated in there because they were apprentices to their mothers. We call them the ash girls. They are forced to labor below, to run the engines and with their wheels and pipes to keep the air cold enough to sustain ice throughout the palace except for certain rooms and corridors. They have been down there, separated from us for all these centuries. We worry over them. The ash girls have unique knowledge, and there are things in that basement that our mothers left behind: mysterious wheels and implements.

"By our wits, we have learned some secrets of the barge. We manage our secret lives here well, but even better since Tom Cavan and his mother have come, because Uria is always listening to them. We have been for a long time insignificant to Uria. Even still, she would sometimes listen to us out of curiosity. But long ago, we developed a language in gestures."

"The goddess doesn't trust Tom Cavan, though she has made him her agent," Wheeta said. "He is doing some kind of work for her, searching for something on-shore. Tom must be doing something to betray her, because he has discovered some of those deaf spots on the ship. He speaks to his mother and sometimes to English soldiers in those areas."

"He pretends to serve Uria, but it seems he has plans of his own," Gudrun agreed.

Tom's presence on the ship made me feel fearful for Mam and Ishleen. I gazed at them. "Are they safe in here?" I asked Gudrun.

"Yes," she said. She then looked sadly and meaningfully at Phee, who hung her head slightly and stared at the icy floor. Whatever it was seemed a private matter, so I didn't ask. But there was another question that was burning in my mind.

"May I ask you, you said that each girl tends to her mother's vacant body?"

Gudrun and Phee exchanged a glance.

"Yes," Gudrun said softly. "They are in the inner sanctum."

They led me through a narrow passage and pushed on a door that swung slowly open with a long despairing groan. I followed them into a very long icy dormitory room, dim and blue, lit by blue flames in sconces on the walls. A multitude of slim white beds were lined up in rows. My heart contracted. On each bed lay the body of a woman, every one in a slightly different posture, some with hair spread out on pillows in frozen clumps, some bodies draped in fabric starched with ice. An occasional bare foot or hand peeked out from under icy drapery, blue with cold.

"Each girl tends to her own mother's body," Gudrun whispered.

I watched a very small girl brush away gathering snow from her mother's hair, then look up at me, wearing an expression of haunted composure.

The walls were spangled in crystals of frost, and snow fell and floated in the dim blueness of the lamps. Deeper inside, a child pushed a shovel between a row of beds, and another followed, dusting salt in the pathways to prevent girls from slipping on the ice.

A small girl held a bit of mirror up to her mother's

mouth, and let out a little relieved sigh to see it misting over.

"When it gets very cold, the heartbeat slows down so much it can be difficult to detect, and girls get panicky, so they use the little mirror to check for breathing. This room is subject to blizzards, and the gusts blow so hard sometimes that they snuff out the lamps, so there are always girls in attendance."

"Can't they be moved to a warmer place?"

"But you see," Wheeta said, "we want them in this very cold room. It preserves them in the state they are in. It is a terrible balancing act we must sustain. The cold will preserve them, but it cannot be so cold that they will lose hold of life."

"Look over here," Gudrun whispered, beckoning near a wall. "This entire dormitory room is part of a wrecked vessel stuck in the ice. We have very carefully created seams in the ice that attaches it to the barge, so that when the right moment arrives one day, it will require only minimum strategic cutting from the wall in order to detach this dormitory from the ship.

"Our plan had once been to release the ghost souls and try to return them to the mothers' bodies. Come here," she whispered, and beckoned me after.

At the end of the dormitory, she drew aside a velvet curtain, stiff with frost, revealing what looked like a large dresser of opaque ice with three semitransparent drawers. Each one contained the body of a woman, each in a posture both stiff and graceful. All three looked as if they'd been caught midswim, frozen.

"Phee, a girl named Lloyda and a girl named Rue had volunteered to release their mothers' ghost souls to see if they could be coaxed back into their bodies. When the souls were released from the ice," Gudrun whispered, watching Phee kneel down before the lowest drawer and peer in, "they dissipated on the air, and the bodies convulsed almost as if they were dancing, and died suddenly."

Phee touched the side of her face to the ice drawer that contained her mother.

"All these centuries later it is still unbearable for her."

I knelt down and looked in at Phee's dark-haired mother, lying on her back, twisted slightly at the waist, neck arched and arms lifted as if she were floating. Her palms faced up, and long strands of hair were petrified, caught forever in a whirl around her head. But the most striking thing about her was the expression on her face, eyes wide open and staring up, almost euphoric.

As Phee touched the ice with her fingertips, I asked Gudrun, "What do you think could have happened to her mother's ghost soul?"

"We believe that Phee breathed in some of her mother's soul, and that accounts for her strange wisdom and unnatural intuition. And we think that particles of the souls that dissipated inhabit the air all around us."

"Yes, and Phee seems to have inherited some of her mother's memories! She knows things from well before she was born," Wheeta added.

"So Phee's mother does live on, in a sense," I said.

"Well, yes," Gudrun whispered. "As all dead mothers

live on in their daughters. But Phee cannot speak to her or even see a spark of her, like the rest of us see our mothers shimmering in the ice.

"The three girls who lost their mothers this way, Phee, Lloyda and Rue, escaped this barge in their despair. They tried to reach the Holy Isles of Danu. They made it into the dark circle of the sea, the Realm of the Shee. But Uria's mermaids brought them back."

Little Phee stood and pushed up the sleeve on one arm, revealing a series of ornate scars in the shape of teeth. My heart filled with sadness and I was overwhelmed with a desire to take her into my arms.

"When the mermaids brought them back, an example was going to be made of them. They were going to be killed," Gudrun said. "But then Phee had a premonition. She signed to me and I translated for the goddess: 'In a bog at the northwestern coast of Ireland, a man will find things you lost in battle.' With her signs, Phee spelled out a name and I said it out loud: Tom Cavan.

The goddess listened and said that the executions of the three girls could be put off. Phee described other things she could *see* about Ard Macha, and Uria, remembering it well as the battleground where she once fell, believed in Phee's clairvoyance. Phee's life was spared, but Uria decided to put Lloyda and Rue to death, and had their bodies thrown into the sea.

"Phee didn't tell the goddess everything about her premonition. She didn't tell her that a young Irish woman would be sent by the Swan Women."

"A young Irish woman?" I asked.

"You," she said. "But all that happened long ago. Since then, we've done nothing outwardly rebellious, and Uria has forgotten us. She and her henchwomen are not suspicious of us.

"Phee had a vision, like the one she'd had about Tom Cavan and about you. In it she saw how dresses could be made with ethereal threads, dresses and veils that could contain each ghost soul and help keep it intact so that it could gradually reenter its original body when the right moment arrives and the souls can be released. We have made ethereal dresses and veils for all of them. Work has already begun on the dresses for your mother and sister. I will show you those soon, but first, I will show you this."

We went through another curtain into the deepest chamber, where she pointed to a similar ice dresser, but this one with five drawers.

"These are the tundra priestesses, the five mothers of the five ash girls who are imprisoned downstairs. They were killed when Uria found them in her lair. Their ghost souls, we believe, dissipated long, long ago."

These regal-looking women, unlike the three others, lay in heavy, still postures, their hands folded on their chests. Each looked solemn and stared straight up, thin ribbons of blood frozen midspill at the corners of their mouths.

We bowed our heads, gazing at them in silence, until Gudrun touched my arm, indicating that we were going.

I followed her, Phee and Wheeta back out through the grim and frozen dormitory, into the front chapel where the ghost souls were kept and through a curtain. On dozens of dress forms hung delicate pale opaque shifts, tiny balls of light dripping occasionally down over each garment and rolling to the floor.

A group of tundra girls, wearing spectacles with lenses of thick crystal, were gathered around a concentration of blue lamps. They squinted at their needles and threads, wizened children bent over delicate work.

The thread they used was barely substantial and, like the dresses, dripped with the occasional tiny pellet of light. One girl swept up a group of these pellets into her hand, squeezed them and then worked them into a single strand of thread.

"When the time comes, we have a vehicle for each of our mothers' ghost souls," Gudrun said. "These are for your mother and sister." She pointed to two dresses being created by a slender long-necked girl in the corner.

"Thank you," I said to the girl as I knelt to look at her work.

The girl took out a long blue needle and a wooden spool.

"She needs to take soul thread from you, Maeve, to make the dresses truly powerful," Gudrun said.

"What do you mean?" I asked.

Before an answer came, the girl inserted the needle into my fingertip, and I felt a tiny sting. In a moment, a very fine, almost invisible thread began to issue out through the hollow of the needle. The girl wound it carefully around the spool.

She nodded at me, blinking several times, her eyes

damp from all the concentrated squinting. A few droplets had frozen into tiny crystals on her eyelashes. She turned away from me and began again to ply her needle.

"When our mothers' ghost souls are free of the ice, these dresses will help them each have a separate image. Their particles will all stay in one place, and the dresses will be their engines of transport," Gudrun said.

"Transport?" I asked.

"Yes. There are many things you don't realize about the power of dresses, especially when they are enhanced by ethereal thread. Each daughter contributes thread from her own soul for her mother's dress. You will learn."

"I will try," I said nervously, afraid at how much they were all depending on me.

"What is the first task you have?" Gudrun asked as we stepped through the curtain again, back into the presence of the ghost souls in ice.

"I am supposed to find Danu's Fire Opal and bring it to her at the Holy Isles."

Phee gestured excitedly to Gudrun.

"The ash girls," she said. "Somehow you must go to them. Phee says they can help you find the Fire Opal."

"How do I do that?" I asked.

Just then we heard a massive boom and crash, as if thousands of pieces of glass were breaking all at once.

Wheeta went out to see and came back quickly. A strong blast of wind had knocked down the chandelier in the empty ballroom.

"You should go back to your room," Gudrun urged.

I looked at Mam and Ishleen pulsing softly behind the facades of ice. I ached to stay longer with them, but Gudrun rushed me out of the chapel. "Someone is bound to come."

I quickly went into the room where I was staying and closed the door.

The blue fire in the grate had dwindled, and one of the coals was whistling. When I looked at the carved face on the mantel, I saw that it had changed its expression, no longer with set teeth as if pronouncing the letter S. The lips were now round and pursed, as if they and not the coal were the source of the whistle. I had the distinct feeling that the face was watching me suspiciously.

I listened hard at the door but heard no one come to inspect, and found that curious. I tried to sleep but felt painfully restless, and finally, in the middle of the night, I got up again, thinking I might go see Mam and Ishleen and listen for the soothing vibrations of their presence. I was crestfallen when I found the chapel door locked. I wandered again through cold, snaking corridors until I found the place where pristine, decoratively carved ice walls and perfectly sheened floors gave way to a dark and primitive passage, the ground dirty slush.

Though my heart was banging so hard that my rib cage shook, something propelled me forward. The sound of Uria's breathing and heartbeat had been steadily amplifying the closer I got, and an unsettling odor, something vaguely rancid, intensified on the frigid air.

Still, a curiosity edged with horror drove me. I pushed on a rough stone door, and it groaned open. The tunnel before me was dim. A silhouette of what looked like some kind of stone embankment about six feet away from me suddenly moved, and I stopped in my tracks. Before I could discern what it was, light issued from five places deeper in the passage: five bodiless human heads were staring wide-eyed at me, frowning and furrowing their brows. Insect legs unfolded from beneath them and they began to move forward—quivering, uncanny spiders.

They halted suddenly as the embankment shifted, and a large, hunched creature turned and looked directly at me. His head was rough and human-looking, but his flesh looked as if it were made of stone—dark, damp marble veined with cloudy white streaks. He breathed audibly and noisily, like an asthmatic, sputtering clouds of condensation issuing from his mouth as he did. He was chained there at the rocks, forced to be a guard at the door of Uria's lair. As he gazed at me, I experienced the shocking certainty that I knew him, and that he also recognized me. For a few moments, he focused on me and did not move. The pity I felt for him in that moment eclipsed my fear of his monstrous form, and I thought that if that moment could have gone on a little longer, I might have figured out who he was.

His lower body shifted suddenly and awkwardly, and he rose up onto four stiff, spindly legs. From the waist up he was a muscular human male, but he had the lower body of a deer or a hind, a kind of bizarre centaur. Standing at his height, he had to struggle to balance himself, but when at last he did, he reared back slightly and opened his mouth wide, his eyeballs rolling. Terror shot through my spine like a needle.

My trespassing clearly disturbed Uria herself. Her breathing grew loud and uneven, and the drumbeat of her heart pounded in my nerves and eardrums.

Somehow I managed to turn and run. When I reached the familiar corridor, I saw doors creaking open and closed. I rushed into my room and shut myself in.

A tiny cold particle hit my cheek, and I turned, trying to find the source. Several more fell and drifted on the air of the room, and soon a snowstorm began all around me, driving down at a slant from some mysterious source.

I got into bed under the canopy and closed the bed curtains around me. Uria's hectic breathing continued. The racing heart would slow down, only to speed up again to a gallop. The hotter her temper, as evident in her breathing and heartbeat, the colder the air.

All at once the breathing and heartbeat came to an abrupt stop. I heard something unidentifiable then that terrified me: a metallic cranking and almost whirring noise that seemed to be approaching from a distant corridor and coming closer and closer, then stopping just outside my door.

I wrapped the blankets around me, shivering violently, my teeth chattering so hard I thought they'd break. After an interminable pause, the loud thing began to clank again and whirr, then continued on its way until I could no longer hear it.

When it felt safe, I moved the curtain and looked out

into the room, the snow flying like furious birds. The face over the mantel wore a surprised smile, as if enjoying the storm. It opened its mouth suddenly and tried to catch a snowflake on its white tongue.

I heard the clanking, squeaking thing return and held my breath as it stopped again outside my door. When at last it continued on its way, I let go a deep sigh, finally recognizing how exhausted I was.

Uria's breathing and heartbeat resumed, at first hectic and loud, and gradually growing calmer. The snow thinned out until only an occasional sparkling fleck wandered the air. White drifts were gathered in every corner, and a thick white blanket covered the floor.

I lay back as the air took on a more temperate climate, and then I sighed deeply and closed my eyes. When I opened them a few hours later, the snow was gone and the floors were damp.

CHAPTER 17

It was Mrs. Cavan who opened the bed curtains in the morning and brought me a tray. I drank the hot tea and ate the warm oatcakes and boiled eggs so quickly that I had to catch my breath when I finished.

The face on the mantel had a placid, vacant look to it, and Uria's breathing was soft—quiet, even—her heartbeat slow and steady. There was clearly no threat on the air, and that heartened me greatly, as if it had all been a passing nightmare.

"I heard that you were wandering around last night," Mrs. Cavan said.

"Yes. I couldn't sleep."

"I don't want you doing that again," she said sternly, and focused threateningly on me. She inhaled deeply through her nostrils. "Come with me! I have ordered dresses to be made for you. The seamstresses have been working on them since before dawn. You need to be fitted, and the hems need to be measured. And, of course, a ceremonial dress is being created for you for tonight's performance of 'The Canticle of Fire,' when you will first be in the presence of Uria's emanation and possibly introduced to her, depending upon her mood."

I followed Mrs. Cavan a long way down a windy corridor. By day, the light was different on the barge, but still drained of the warmer colors, as if the spectrum in this world of ice could not include them. A cool, glimmering sun outside penetrated the ice walls, so a hallucinatory light imbued with pale blue flooded the interiors.

"It's getting too warm around the barge," Mrs. Cavan said. "Soon it will enshroud itself with cold fog."

"How does it do that?"

"Through the engine. The entire barge is carefully regulated from within."

I thought of the mysterious ash girls below.

She opened a large door and beckoned me into a more shadowy region of the barge, where four form-fitting long-sleeved shifts stood on dressmakers' forms, each at various stages of completeness.

All were lovely at first glance, but as I moved among them, I felt a shiver of dread. Only one, the palest of the lot, a dull golden yellow imbued in gray, looked complete.

I approached it warily, uncertain what about it and its unfinished sisters made me uneasy. Gudrun appeared from between two curtains at the back of the room.

"Why is only one dress finished?" Mrs. Cavan asked with a note of accusation in her voice.

"I was trying to work on the ceremonial dress for tonight. I need the young lady for a few minutes for a fitting."

"All right, then," Mrs. Cavan said impatiently. "I'll go and see to Tom, and then I'll come back for her. After the fitting, make sure she puts on the finished dress." She pointed to the dull ochre-gray.

Gudrun beckoned me to follow her through the curtains, where the dress I had made stood in the process of being embellished and added to. Gudrun's additions had made it appear even more like the metallic dress in Muldoon's.

"I want to speak to you," Gudrun said in an urgent half whisper. "Don't worry. Uria's not listening."

"How do you know?"

"I can hear it in the rhythms of her breathing. And when she is listening directly, you always know by the pulse of her heart, which you can feel just perceptibly as if it were under your own skin.

"The dress must be completely in tune with you," she said. "As a seal is one with its thick, glistening fur, and a swan is one with her feathers and her wings, so should a woman be with her garment. This dress, which you must wear for every important action in Danu's name, must serve as your mode of navigation, your engine of transport.

"I am making a special pocket in which to hide the Fire Opal."

We could hear the juddering echoes of Mrs. Cavan's returning footsteps.

"Quick," Gudrun whispered. "I just want to warn you about those other dresses she ordered for you."

I followed her back through the curtains and into the presence of the disquieting dresses.

"She gave specifications. . . . They are all supposed to be dresses of oppression. This finished one," she said, pointing to the dull golden yellow, "is the least cruel. That's why I completed it first. The fabric is imbued with certain tinctures meant to keep you disoriented. Mrs. Cavan is looking for ways to hold a constant advantage over you. Clearly, she doesn't trust you."

She pointed to each of the others, every one a darker gray than the one before it. "This dress is meant to constrict your breathing, and this one is meant to make you lethargic. The last one is the worst of all. It is meant to erase your memory."

"Erase my memory," I repeated. "Why would she want to do that?"

Mrs. Cavan's footsteps were now echoing closer.

"Put on the finished one. Don't worry. Just try to keep your concentration as best as you can."

Before I took off my dress I remembered the piece of mirror and Francisco's compass in the pocket. I took them out and slipped them into the pocket of the dull ochre dress, which Gudrun quickly helped me into. When Mrs. Cavan entered the room, Gudrun was busy fastening the back.

"Be sure these others are finished soon," Mrs. Cavan said coldly to Gudrun, who bowed her head in response.

Stepping after Mrs. Cavan into the corridor, I immediately felt a wave of disorientation. I had to stop and lean with one arm against the icy wall to get my bearings.

Mrs. Cavan turned and focused on me with a fascinated satisfaction.

"The dress is a little tight," I said.

"You just need to wear it awhile and it will adjust, I am sure."

As I walked, the ground moved beneath my feet. The strange bluish pallor of everything was intensified by daylight. Shadows seemed to fall at suspicious angles. I turned once to look behind me and saw the corridors receding, as if the room we had exited only moments before was now a great distance away. Space seemed to shift unpredictably in this place.

We stopped at an open door.

"Go to him," she said, and pushed me in. It was the room of the awful tableau, the bodies of the Spaniards behind ice. Tom Cavan stood dramatically in the middle of the space with his back to me, holding two little black iron boxes. I walked in slowly, each hesitant footstep echoing my reluctance on the polished ice floor, and stopped about a yard away from him. I sensed Uria listening expectantly, her breathing arrhythmic with long spells of quiet, and I could feel the pulse of her heartbeat as if in my own body.

Tom turned suddenly and faced me, elegantly attired

in his long velvet jacket with tails, white lace cuffs and a white lace cravat. His wavy hair had grown long and blew to one side in the gusts.

In spite of myself, I saw with a shock what other girls must have seen when they looked at him. He was extremely handsome, almost unnaturally so. Maybe if he had stayed completely still, if he had not spoken, that spell would have lasted longer and I might have held back my breath in reluctant admiration. But he moved and then he spoke.

"Welcome to your new home, Maeve."

The sound of his voice flooded me with every terrible memory associated with him. I started to shake; my dislike, even hatred, of him overtook me. The floor moved and I swayed on my feet, and, even though I was cold, sweat broke out on my temples. I fought these waves of disorientation. The idea of submitting to him went against every nerve in my body.

"My mother told me that she advised you against asking questions." His voice had an authoritative echo to it, and I realized that he was much taller than he'd been when I'd last seen him. I wondered if my senses were tricking me and this was all the effect of the dress, or if he had actually managed to gain height. He looked well over six feet tall. When I'd last seen him in Ard Macha, he'd been only about five foot ten.

"She doesn't want you to be curious, but I think it's good. I want to tell you everything so that you understand the kind of power I have here."

I kept my eyes averted from his, feeling gripped by a wave of disorientation. This awful dress, I thought.

"It flatters you nicely," he said as if reading my thoughts. I glanced at him. His eyes were tracing the contours of my form. His gloating, self-satisfied smile caused a rush of angry blood to heat my face. I discovered, to my relief and surprise, that the feeling of anger dispelled some of the disorientation.

He kept smiling as he gazed at me. "You know I've always been drawn to the fire in you. It's always been my passion to see you blush and shake with frustration."

He stared blatantly now, his eyes wide and his mouth slightly open with expectation, enthralled by any trace of my anger expressing itself.

Another wave of rage washed away more disorientation. I found that it was better if unexpressed and only felt. This way it did more powerful work.

He watched me with a dark, intrigued smile. Again, I was struck by his beauty. He seemed in his element in this cold light. I averted my eyes again.

It occurred to me now that he might have known that the oppressive dress would inspire anger in me, and that I would be smart enough to discover that the anger was an antidote to the poisonous spell the dress exuded.

"Why were you with English soldiers last night?" I asked.

He focused on me and seemed to be considering whether or not he should answer.

"Do you see all these figures behind the ice?" he asked.

"Spaniards from the armada ships. We have here the bodies of almost every Spaniard who tried to defeat the English in the Irish Sea."

"So you are in league with the English invaders? You are a traitor against Ireland, happy to kill our Spanish allies?" The floor and everything around me was rock solid, absolutely still, and my senses clear.

He stared at me with an uncertain smile. Then he opened a door that led out onto the deck and pointed at three vulture women perched on the rail. Others floated serenely in the air above the barge.

"Uria's ladies, as I call them, swarmed the corpses and siphoned the ghost souls. It's a talent they have, siphoning souls out of bodies, living or dead."

I was about to break in and accuse him of orchestrating this violence against my own mother and sister, but he cut me off.

"You remember the first ship that crashed? We brought the three men still alive to my mother's cottage. One of those men you started fawning over, a kind of dark gypsy." He stared at me, feigning a laugh.

My heart lurched with fear that he had Francisco's body here somewhere. "Where is that man? Is he in the ice?" I demanded.

He narrowed his eyes at me. "No, he isn't here, but the ladies are intent on finding him. He can't have gone far. We have many of the others from the ship he was on." He pointed vaguely at the wall. "In a way, it's your fault. Perhaps if you hadn't mooned over him, I'd not have advised Uria that every Spanish life be taken. So you see, many of these dead are your fault. Some of them, perhaps many of them, on the ships that followed that first one might have been spared, but you had to fawn over that gypsy. . . ." He paused and glared at me.

Then he approached me slowly. The chandeliers chimed above, a weird, inhuman-sounding music. He put his arm slowly around me, one hand pressed to my waist. Containing my fury and upset, I trembled hard, and he gazed with intent fascination at me. He took my hand and, accompanied by the bright, dissonant twangs of the chandeliers, led me in a dance.

I moved stiffly, but when he breathed in my hair, I couldn't bear it and turned my head quickly away.

"You are responsible for my mother and sister!" I disentangled my hand from his and stepped away from him. "I saw them last night."

"You are free to see them whenever you like. Every ice carving with light in it is a ghost. Most are the ghost souls of the dead, but some, like your mother and sister, are still living. Eventually their abandoned bodies will die, but their ghosts will live on to illuminate the barge. That light can burn eternally for us if we allow it to."

"You're talking about the souls of my mother and sister," I cried, and the anger I could not help but express caused him to come close to me again.

"What you should realize, Maeve, is that I am offering you eternity and power."

"I don't want those things," I said. "Especially not with you."

At this, a dark look washed over his features. "If you

do anything that truly displeases me, I can have your mother's and sister's ghost souls placed in these black iron boxes where they will be perpetually isolated and in complete darkness."

"You wouldn't do that," I said.

"I would," he sneered softly.

"Well, then, I would have to fight back somehow."

Something occurred to him, a serious thoughtful look coming into his eyes. He took my arm and steered me through a hallway, unlocking a heavy door that led to a staircase down into a dark, cold basement.

"She can't hear us here. You must never meet with Uria privately. Only when I am with you."

"Why?" I asked.

"Never mind why. Just don't do it or I will put your mother and sister in these." He held up the small iron boxes.

From his tone it was clear that he did not trust Uria. I was pleased at this revelation of vulnerability in him, though I did not yet know how I might make use of it.

All of a sudden, a door creaked open below. A little ragamuffin of a girl covered in blue ashes came out, one of her feet dragging a chain.

She peered up at us quietly and then said, "I've come out for more ghost matter."

Tom smiled. "Let me show you, Maeve, what is done with the ghosts of the Spaniards. Come here."

I had assumed that the ash girls, being apprentices to their mothers, would be at least Gudrun's age, but all these girls were tiny, gaunt and large-eyed, dull blue ash and sweat soiling their colorful hats and dresses, tufts of the matted fur linings peeking out from beneath their sleeves and skirts. Ashes coated their faces and forearms, and the dim steamy room of their prison was cobalt-blue with light from an oven kept ajar. All manner of metal wheels and pipes, things that looked like mystical contraptions, filled the area.

"Show this young lady how the engines work," Tom said.

One of them turned a metal wheel, and a large round container funneled light into a complicated network of pipes, releasing steam. Pistons lifted and huffed mechanically.

"The ghost souls of males provide energy," Tom said. "Those of females provide illumination, so that is what is harvested from each. This container we keep filled with male ghost matter. The ghosts feed the pistons with their energy, and the temperature and life force of the barge is controlled. The cold winds and icy conditions are channeled throughout on air currents that originate here. This barge maintains its own weather systems, and these girls are responsible for keeping it working. Of course, they have no choice but to do it. If they didn't, the ice all around the mothers upstairs would melt.

"Uria has always harvested ghost souls as food and energy and light, but the armada ships provided a windfall."

My mind worked wildly as I tried to think of ways I might find private words with these little ash girls, but like Gudrun and Phee, they recognized me for who I might be: one approached, wide-eyed, and showed me her hands covered in burns from scorching cold.

"This little girl needs help. Look at her hands!" I went to my knees before her, taking her hands gently and peering into her eyes. "I demand beeswax to rub into these burns."

Tom smiled, entertained by my desire to help, the way he had been when I'd held the dying baby bird he had knocked from its nest years ago.

"My friends, too, need caring for," the child said in a soft voice, and all of them crowded me, showing me their burns.

"You haven't changed, Maeve," Tom said. "Still wasting energy on the insignificant pests of the world. Forget about the beeswax."

"If you won't get the beeswax for me, I will ask Uria herself for it," I said.

His face dropped.

"I will go directly to her and speak to her. If every small request I have"—I paused for effect—"*as a wife* is going to be refused, I imagine that I might often have to go to Uria."

The words worked some kind of magic on him. "I will get you the beeswax," he said plainly.

"And I would like to take the time I need to treat each little girl."

"All right, but I warn you, you must never have a private conversation with Uria."

I did not pursue this. It intrigued me that he felt no

threat at all from the ash girls. He seemed to have no idea of their history.

"I will be back to help you," I said to the girls as Tom led me out. "And they shouldn't be chained," I told him.

"They will stay chained," he answered. "And if anything goes wrong, you will be working the pistons and wheels with them."

As we ascended the stairs, he grabbed my arm, then pushed me back against the wall, coming close and staring down at me. I wriggled away from him, then turned my back on him, but I felt his eyes on me and they seemed to heat the exposed skin at the back of my neck. He came close.

"If you cause any problems, you know what will happen to your mother's and sister's ghosts."

Shaking, I said, "I ask you, Tom Cavan, with all this hatred you feel for me, why do you want to marry me?"

"I don't feel hatred for you, Maeve. This is how I love."

His voice dropped a couple of decibels, and he said, "It's about upsetting you, Maeve." He stroked my waist and ran his hand up my back, moving my hair away from my neck. "And about frustrating you so that I can see the fireworks in your face. That warms me like nothing else ever has."

CHAPTER 18

 was forced to spend most of the day under Mrs.
Cavan's oppressive, watchful eye. She knitted, and insisted I do the same. The ice-cold needles never seemed
to warm from the friction of my hands.

I asked several times if I might take off the ochre dress
and lie down. She said I could lie down but that I'd have
to keep the dress on.

In the late afternoon, I was lying on my side on the
bed, biding my time with the disorienting effects of the
dress, when one of Uria's vulture "ladies" appeared at
the door with a jar of beeswax and conferred quietly with
Mrs. Cavan.

"Go with her," Mrs. Cavan instructed me.

The vulture woman led me through the frosty
labyrinthine corridors of the barge, and unlocked the

heavy door to the basement. She handed me the beeswax and let me through, but did not follow, closing the door behind me with a boom.

I was halfway down the stairs when the little girl who had come out earlier appeared again, the heavy chain causing her to limp and lurch slightly. I entered the cold deeply blue basement, and the chained creatures crowded around me and told me their names. The girl who had first come out was Breeze. Her cousins, all frail-looking in their ashy clothes and all with dull shadows beneath their large, brimming eyes, were called Trillip, Trala, Floreen and Faze.

"You are sent by the Swan Women," Breeze said.

"Yes," I replied, "and I am looking for something under their instruction. The tundra girls upstairs told me that you might be able to tell me how to find the large Fire Opal that belongs to Danu."

There was a grave collective silence, which filled me with unease.

"What is the significance of the Fire Opal?" I asked.

Breeze went very thoughtful, then shook her head. "We don't know. Our mothers knew, we believe. It was what they were trying to get when they were caught."

"It's a very dangerous task," the girl named Trillip said in a soft, barely audible voice.

"We have heard that it is very beautiful," Breeze said dreamily. "Red and orange, like true fire."

"And flecked with tiny spots of bright green," Trillip said with a quiver of excitement.

Breeze took a pair of long iron tongs and reached into

the back of the glowing forge. From the crumbs of blue ember and ash, she extricated what looked like a blue glowing coal.

"We think the Fire Opal must look a little like this, only much larger and the color of true fire. Our mothers gave us each a small Fire Opal similar in nature to Danu's, but these have been fed only false fire, so they are bluish now."

She set it carefully on the flat iron of the range and told me to wait. Wisps of slow voluptuous blue-green smoke rose from it.

"You must wonder how we've survived with our spirits intact all these centuries, trapped in this room." Breeze touched the opal, testing to see if it was cool, and when she felt it was, she extended it to me. "We each keep one in our pocket at night and hold it and breathe on it. Try it."

As I breathed on the opal, Breeze touched my arm, and the air and light around us stirred with particles, green and gold and flashing. Suddenly I no longer found myself in the cold, steamy blue basement filled with arcane wheels and defunct mechanisms but in a dense, atmospheric forest echoing with birdsong. Breeze was there at my side, but the other girls were nowhere to be seen.

The trees were so large and high that they created a green canopy over us, so it was as if we were inside and outside at once, the air fragrant with leaves and flowers.

"These are the oak trees that once composed the sacred groves and primeval forests of Ireland. But because we have only false fire, we experience it all as if we are seeing it through darkened glass."

There was a cast to everything, a brightness missing, but still, I could understand how visits to this rich, strange place kept these girls from total despair.

On the trunks and branches of the oak trees, mistletoe grew in thick swags, emitting sharp aromatic evergreen fragrances, the luminous berries hanging in damp clumps like pearls.

Breeze glanced significantly at the trunk of one of the oak trees. I jumped slightly when I saw a male figure emerging from the bark. The more he came forward from the tree, the more solid and separate from it his visage became, until he stood almost completely separate, the skin of his strong arms and chest a velvety green, his hair a paler, more golden green. He peered at me and gave me a smile, partly curious, partly mischievous. Then he retreated suddenly, merging back into the tree until he was no longer visible.

"We are all descended from such creatures. The world was once filled with animation, Maeve. The earth, air, water and fire of Ireland were once intensely fertile realms."

I followed Breeze through a maze rampant with wildflowers and ivy, and upon turning a corner became aware of a ghostlike image forming itself a few feet before us. I stopped in my tracks and watched the subtle impression of a female figure defining itself. The body never fully took form, but the face resolved itself, and she studied me with as much curiosity as the green man of the tree had.

"The air and the wind have elementals as well," Breeze explained.

The transparent young woman looked more and more palpable before shivering there and dissolving, leaving a trace of smoke. As Breeze and I continued on our way, I passed through the air in which the elemental had just stood, and breathed a warm fragrance like incense from an exotic wood.

"We should go back," she said, and as she extended the opal away from her body, the forest around us disappeared.

"The large Fire Opal belongs to Danu and is the last of its kind," she explained as we found ourselves again in the ice-cold blue dungeon. "It contains the potential of an entire primeval forest, with all the original laws of nature in place."

"Do you know where it is?"

The girls exchanged uneasy looks. "Yes. It is in Uria's lair. Yours is the same quest that our mothers were on and were destroyed for undertaking. The most dangerous thing that you can do is venture into Uria's lair. You see, she cannot bear to be seen in her true shame."

"Her shame?"

"Uria's true body lies in there, cocooned and preserved in ice and wax and amber. She still bears the burns she suffered in battle with Danu seven centuries ago. To preserve her life, she never leaves that cocoon, though she has developed an emanation, as you know. It travels out from the lair connected to her cocooned body by a fleshy cord. The emanation is filled with air like a balloon, and is only held down by traveling in an iron dress on a metal platform with wheels."

The memory of the clanking, squeaking noise sent a shiver through me. I stared into the blue light of the forge.

Two of the little girls opened the jar of beeswax and, dipping their fingers into it, began rubbing it on their tiny hands.

They looked up at me with large eyes, and I could not help marveling at the fact that they were each ancient beings wearing auras of wisdom, yet they were orphans, huddling together, yearning and blighted.

Noticing the way I was observing them, Breeze said, "We've wondered what it is in the nature of the blue air in this barge that keeps us stuck. It is awful to live on this way, all of us in the thrall of our grief and longing for our mothers, but perhaps the one good thing is that we remember so far into the past."

"They keep you so isolated down here," I said.

A very little one, named Trala, with a pointed, upturned nose, spoke.

"Uria and her henchwomen have gradually made themselves more and more distant from this engine works and this forge. The light down here is brighter, and blinding to them. It all stems from Uria's fear of fire."

Now they all took turns chiming in. "You see," said Floreen, who had very dark eyes, "because true fire was once down here, she is afraid that it might ignite again, that there might be an ash somewhere, an ember very gray but still volatile."

"That is how obsessed she is!" exclaimed Trala.

"The women leave the ghost matter in the vats, and we are to gather it and are supposed to channel it into the engine to make the pistons run," explained Faze, whose face was covered with streaks of blue ash.

"But they do not know that for centuries we have not done that. And the barge has now been stationary here for years, at anchor in the same place," Breeze said. "We do not need the ghost matter to keep the ship working."

"That's right," Trillip piped up, looking at me with earnest eyes. "We burn the inordinate amount of garbage that Uria and her ladies create, and that is enough to power this barge."

"And even to keep the temperatures regulated in the various chambers," Floreen said. "But none of the vulture women even thinks of such things. They leave the mysteries of the barge to us and have forgotten everything about how it works."

"We have saved the souls of every Spaniard," Breeze told me proudly. "Tom Cavan thinks they are being used for fuel, but he is wrong. Every ghost lives on, and we are just trying to find a way to release them."

"We think there is a very high window," Floreen said, pointing up into a dim corner of the room. "There is far too much ice over it, and it is too distant for us to reach in our chains."

"I will help you," I said.

I stacked several wheels and dilapidated pieces of metal in the designated corner and stood on them, finding myself within easy reach of the window. "Give me something to use to chip away at the ice," I instructed.

Trillip and Trala moved through the area of the room littered with metal pipes, bars and rusted wheels. Trala found a kind of iron hammer and chisel and handed them to me. I began to hit the ice, but made loud noises each time I did, so I stopped, frightened that the sound would travel into the upper floors of the barge and cause suspicion.

I squinted and strained my eyes, peering through the thick ice.

"Yes, the sky is there," I said. "This window is just above water level. If we could somehow melt this ice . . ."

I stared at it, wishing I could hit it hard and crack it. Then, in my mind's eye, I remembered Fingal angling the broken piece of mirror onto the dry beach grass, starting a tiny fire.

I reached into the depths of my pocket and withdrew the broken piece of mirror.

"Can one of you find a small bit of something dry like wood or paper?" I asked.

Trala looked among the ashes and broken pipes, found a piece of brittle wood about a foot long, and handed it up to me.

"Can someone hold a lit candle up as high as possible over here?" I asked.

Breeze brought the candle, holding it high, the blue flame close enough to me for the purpose I had in mind.

With my left hand, I held one end of the piece of dry wood a few inches from the flame, while with my right hand I angled the mirror so it reflected the light. In certain positions, the light flashed brilliantly in the mirror. My heart raced when bands of color, a range of all blues into purple, appeared.

Focusing on the purple light, I angled the mirror just right, moving it minutely, until I perceived a very slender thread of red light. I sustained the angle of the mirror and the red light swelled, refracting more and more brightly, until the brittle wood ignited suddenly with true red-orange fire. The ash girls gasped.

I put the mirror away and held the piece of wood to the ice like a torch.

The fire, as if in magical league with us, formed a circle around the window, and the ice dripped away. Breeze waited with a small cup to catch the fire, to keep some of it alive when the rest went out.

Soon I was dismantling big opaque chunks of ice and managed to dislodge the glass from the window. I got down and brought the vat of lit, pulsating ghost matter close to the window. The girls opened the vat, releasing floating figures of light, the sound of many individuals taking in deep breaths. Glowing spinal columns appeared and remained on the air, with very faint images of men forming around them. The ghosts floated there, orienting themselves on the air.

"*La Luz,*" one of them whispered, and they all began whispering different words in Spanish. "*Santa Rita, La Madre de la Luz, Santa Maria.*"

"The names of their ships," I explained to the girls, who looked puzzled. "Up there," I said, pointing to the window that led outside. The ghosts gazed at all of us in recognition, whispering *"Gracias"* and bowing their barely visible heads. A few times, I saw a pumping heart appear to one side of a spine and illuminate with sudden floods of bright rushing particles before fading.

"Nuestra Señora de la Soledad," several whispered at once as they passed me.

"You know Francisco?" I asked.

"Sí," one answered.

"Is he here?"

"No."

"Where is he?"

"No sé. No sé."

Each bent to fit through the window and began swimming on the air. I got up on the stacked wheels and metal again to watch them glowing on the evening air awhile before they moved away, many of them wearing ghostly forms of the jacket Francisco had worn. My heart was battered with remorse when I thought of the one I'd lost.

I lifted the little girls one by one and held them up high, so that they could watch the procession of brilliant spines glowing in the twilight like traveling candles.

When the last one was too far away to see, we all sat in a circle and talked.

"I have to devise a way to get the Fire Opal. There is going to be a reception tonight. Tom Cavan has said that Uria will be there."

"That will be her emanation," Breeze said.

"Do you think the emanation might wear the Fire Opal?" I asked.

"No," they all chimed, shaking their heads.

I explained about the narcotic pastille that the Swan Woman had given me, and told them what she had suggested.

"Yes. I have an idea," Breeze said. "We can burn it down here and send the smoke through the air current during the singing of 'The Canticle of Fire.' This way, anyone, including any guards Uria has around her lair and even her mermaids, who will be gathered on the low deck to hear the singing, will be affected."

"Once I get the Fire Opal, if I can manage it, I am supposed to take a small boat into the western sea and try to find the Holy Isles." But I felt uneasy about the plan. "I'm worried that some won't be in the range of the pastille smoke and they will catch me."

"Oh, don't worry. Absolutely everyone on the barge listens to 'The Canticle of Fire,' " said Breeze.

"Why?" I asked.

Breeze peered into my eyes. "It stirs a kind of nostalgia in everyone who hears it. It must be in our nature to long for our true origins, even someone as corrupt as Uria herself. Although, without compassion in one's nature, listening to it is only a kind of lonely indulgence."

"What if the smoke doesn't work on Uria's body in the ice cocoon? How would I dare trespass to search for the Fire Opal?"

"If one of the Swan Women gave you this pastille, it

will have power over Uria," Floreen said, and all the others chorused their agreement.

"As soon as you see her and everyone else dozing off, follow the fleshy cord from beneath the emanation's dress. It will lead you to her lair," said Breeze.

I gave them pieces of the leaf and told them to eat them before burning the pastille. I left them all gathered in a flurry of whispers around the cup of true fire.

CHAPTER 19

he finished ceremonial dress was extraordinary, much more formidable than the soft metal dress in Muldoon's, and unapologetically armored with little metal platelets in areas around the chest, waist and hips, including numerous small compartments made of tin.

As Gudrun helped me into it, I told her everything that had transpired with Tom Cavan and the ash girls, then breathlessly explained the plan.

"Shouldn't I have something to replace the opal with, just in case it's obvious that it's missing?" I asked.

"Take one of those large crystals from the chandelier that fell," Gudrun suggested. "One the size of an apple, because that is how large the Fire Opal is."

We heard two sets of footsteps approaching from a distant corridor. "We have only a few minutes before they get here and Uria starts to listen," Gudrun said hurriedly. "I was thinking that you should take Phee with you into the western sea. She knows her way through those waters of the Shee, where you will be in danger."

The footsteps stopped just outside in the corridor. Without speaking, Gudrun showed me a deep pocket in the soft, attenuated skirts just at my belly, made specifically, I knew, to hide the Fire Opal. Quickly I slipped her a tiny piece of the antidote leaf.

She seemed to want to share something about the dress, and was about to whisper to me when Tom cleared his throat outside the door. Gudrun pointed at the hems, but immediately dropped her hand and stepped back as Tom came brusquely through the curtain.

He stared at me with wide eyes and a smile growing slowly across his face. Then he grabbed my arm and pulled me after. "Let's go."

I was flanked by Tom and his mother as we walked a long, circuitous path to the ceremonial room, a way I had never gone. I tried to take note of every right and left turn, and found myself astonished by the many empty, elegant rooms the barge contained.

Finally, we reached two great doors thrown wide open onto a large icy room well lit with lamps and candles. Vulture women were lighting flat dishes of incense on stands in each corner. I heard the same terrifying mechanical clanking from the night before. Uria's emanation, a figure about ten feet tall, was entering on a metal platform with wheels, wearing a metal gown. She had high cheekbones and a falcon's gaze. Her metal dress had none of the delicacy of the one I wore, and was brazenly armored, its iron sleeves formed to look like powerfully muscular arms. Uria's emanation clenched her metal fists open and closed and seemed to be concentrating, her brow furrowed, her eyes narrowed.

There was a striking difference between the heavy solidity of her armor and the insubstantiality of her face and neck, which deepened and dissolved, like something both there and not there. A few times, she seemed to stop concentrating, and her emanation under the dress trembled and shook slightly like it was filled with air and not subject to gravity. Without the weighty metal of her garment, that airy emanation might have escaped upward like a balloon.

Though there had been an attempt to hide it with curtains, I could see the fleshy cord, part of it disappearing into shadow. Several times, Uria's eyes flashed in my direction, then looked immediately away, and though I sensed her strong awareness of my presence, she refused to address me.

Through a side entrance, more vulture women were entering, transforming themselves as they came. As humans, their shoulders remained hunched up high, and their heads hung low and oddly forward from their necks, reminiscent of their bird forms. Their yellow eyes, darting and suspicious, raked the shadows of the room. As they took seats, I saw Uria's face deepen and clarify. At that moment, a fanfare began.

Nighttime darkness filled the vast room, and twinkling snowflakes wheeled and swirled all around. I saw the curtain near the floor move, the cord of flesh undulating and coming momentarily into the light. It quivered, riddled with veins and flecked with blood.

Uria lifted an arm, and a simulation of the northern lights began in the air all around us. The vulture women oohed and aahed. Then, lifting her other arm and pointing a trembling finger, Uria caused storm clouds to congregate and flash near the ceiling. I was numb with amazement, swept into the spirit of the grand theatrics. When the clouds were cleared, the room went a deep, dusky blue. The tundra girls all filed in and began to sing, a sweet high-pitched song in a strange language filled with *shhhs* and *chhhs*, lilting ocean sounds. At first the song was quietly poignant, but it built in tension and volume until it was wild with longing. The pitch-perfect voices infused the tissues of my mind and heart, and tears spilled from my eyes. I ached for Mam and Ishleen, for my da and my brothers and for Ard Macha itself, as if it were a distant country I might never make my way back to.

Tom Cavan was looking at me, impatient with my display of emotion, as if it suggested I was too far away from him or not enough under his control. I was not sure what made him so irritated with my tears. Then he reached into his jacket and pulled out the two small iron boxes.

The horror that must have appeared on my features made him smile. He was the cause of that emotion in me, and that must have been what gratified him. Then, to deepen the insult, he slowly traced my arm with his index finger as if he owned me. I pulled away from him, my heart pounding now with anger, and that served to deepen the resolve I felt about the task ahead of me. I reached into the pocket where I'd hidden the antidote leaf and as unobtrusively as possible put it into my mouth and swallowed it.

The woodsy-smelling incense that had been burning suddenly took on a new note, something flowery and cloying, almost overwhelming. The narcotic began to work, and heads were lolling, falling into slumber. Tom and his mother, along with most of Uria's henchwomen, dropped with thudding reverberations to the floor, causing interminable echoing booms.

Uria's emanation was fading, but managed to gather herself momentarily, her fleshy cord stretching and twisting convulsively as if in attempted revolt. She looked directly and knowingly at me, and for a terrifying second, all the light in the room was sucked into the vortex of her eyes. But then those eyes fell closed, and her metal dress opened like a trapdoor from which the emanation rose, drifting weightless and limp to the ceiling; the fleshy cord was the only thing keeping her slightly weighted in her floating.

I climbed over Tom's and his mother's bodies, and the bodies of all the others, careful as I moved through the tundra girls, and followed the fleshy cord on the floor, where it snaked out of the room and down numerous corridors. My breaths were coming in great, audible gusts. As carefully as I could, I peeked into the vestibule that led to Uria's lair.

This close to the source, Uria's heartbeat and breathing were deafening and reverberating, though her heart sounded slow and irregular and her breathing broken and uneven. The strange centaur, lying with his mouth open and his eyes half closed, twitched when he saw me but could not seem to make himself move. When his eyes glazed over, and I knew he was completely unconscious, I struggled past him, still not fully trusting that he wouldn't suddenly revive, and was as deeply struck as I had been the last time by the familiarity of his face. The spiders lay in a stupor, their mouths open and eyes sunken, though each time one of their legs trembled, I jumped.

I pushed open a door of ice into a cave hung with icicles and lit cold blue with fires burning in three hanging lamps. I kept following the cord of flesh, now as thick as the middle of my body, until I saw where it originated, growing like the trunk of a huge vine from out of a kind of pond or icy cocoon. In this frozen and partially petrified tomb of ice, wax and amber, the very large figure of a woman lay, reminiscent of the emanation with her high cheekbones, her sharp falcon's nose and brows. But it was her eyes that caused every nerve and sinew in my body to vibrate. They were very pale blue spheres, cloudy and marbled, staring in frozen horror at me and through me.

She wore archaic platelets of armor similar to the emanation's metal dress, though these were broken and many were missing pieces, the clothing beneath torn and twisted into ropy fabric, partly destroyed. Wounds were visible, red and swollen, as if she had just fallen at battle.

I felt faint when I saw that the walls around the tomb were pulsing and appeared to be made of flesh, red and riddled with capillaries and veins.

And there it was, the large Fire Opal, right at her chest and sewn and held in place by the torn fabric and ropy threads. Everything was frozen except for the area around the Fire Opal, which gave off a gentle heat, the ice there partially melted. I struggled to work the opal free of the dress, the water around it so cold my fingers ached and burned, pulsating stiffly as if they might fall off. Finally I extricated the opal carefully, managing to release it while keeping in place the threads that had caged it. Once I had the opal, I put it into the special pocket and took out the chandelier crystal to replace it.

The cord of flesh suddenly spasmed, hurling itself against the wall, as primitive as a snake, sensing distress. But it lost strength and fell weightless again to the floor.

I rushed from the lair. The guardian chimera stirred and my heart stopped with terror. The cord, which was blocking my way out, lifted as I was climbing over it and violently hurled me against a wall of ice. For a few moments, I was confused, struggling to get my bearings again. The cord collapsed then like dead weight, and I climbed over it and escaped.

"The Canticle of Fire" echoed in my memory with such clarity, it was as if I had heard it hundreds of times before. It had entered my bloodstream and my psyche. As I was passing the chapel of the frozen mothers, I could not resist stepping in to see Mam and Ishleen. The soft light of their ghosts flashed as I approached. In that moment, with the Fire Opal warm against my belly, I could feel so clearly their perpetual state of terror and uncertainty.

"Mam. Ishleen," I uttered. "Don't worry. I'm going to bring you back."

I knew they couldn't understand me, so I said it again several times, hoping they could feel the meaning of my words from my tone. They pulsed and shimmered, and all the mothers in the room began to flash and pulsate, as if they, too, could feel the spirit of what was happening.

"I will help you all," I said, then rushed out and back to the main room, where I found Phee among the others. I lifted her in one arm.

As I descended the staircase to the lower level, I heard the waves murmur and the loose ice on the rough edges of the barge tinkle and groan.

We reached the docks and lower courtyard, where misshapen mermaids lay in openmouthed slumber, icy tides foaming in their hair. A small boat bobbed, tethered to a dock post in a lane of water, and I set my sights on it.

I put Phee down into the boat and had begun to untether the rope from the post when I heard a convulsive sloshing and splashing. Looking up, I saw a rogue mermaid swimming in from the surrounding water, having been out of the range of the narcotic air. She sputtered and growled, baring her teeth as she sped toward me.

I grabbed Phee, and in my struggle to run back toward

the stairs, twisted and ripped the hem of my dress. All at once, the fabric buzzed and vibrated, lifting me into the air up and over the sea, until I saw a little empty boat detached and idling on the waves. My father's boat: *Mananan's Vessel*.

With one arm extended, I parachuted slowly down and landed with Phee in the familiar vessel.

Part Four

Beyond the Horizon

CHAPTER 20

Phee and I sailed deep into the night, the compass with the shattered window keeping us on course. Dawn flooded the sky, clouds broken with red and light that gradually grew dimmer until it cast brooding dark green shadows on air and water.

The Fire Opal, hidden in the folds of my skirts, exuded warmth against my belly. I could just barely hear music, slow and high-pitched, that delicate echoing choir of voices harmonizing in minor keys: "The Canticle of Fire." Sometimes as I listened to it, I rubbed my face, focusing hard, and it stopped abruptly. This made me think that I was hearing it in my own head. But when I forgot about it, it was there again, like hallucinations of sound.

Gradually Phee awakened, and I explained to her that

Gudrun had told me to bring her because she was familiar with the waters of the Shee. She looked around in amazement, her wide-open eyes filled with reflections of the waves as they moved and lifted. When she looked directly at me, I could see my own silhouette.

Hours passed in this extended greenish dawn. The music played and dissolved, a backdrop to the noise of the boat chopping through water and the low roar of the swells beneath us. I lay back, pressing my hands over the pocket that held the Fire Opal, and watched the clouds shift and move. I took the opal out and lifted it, gazing into its rich red-orange transparency flecked with brilliant green, and saw the faces of my father and brothers. The boat seemed to breathe under my back, moving purposefully forward as if navigated by ghosts.

I let Phee hold the Fire Opal. Peering into it, she saw the face of her mother looking very much alive, smiling at her before dissolving into red.

When she returned it to me, just before I put it back into the safe pocket, I saw Francisco's image in it. He was wearing my father's oatmeal-colored shirt, standing somewhere on a cliff gazing off into the distance. The sight of him caused my heart to skip. But unlike Phee's mother, who seemed to look through the opal and see her, Francisco remained unaware of me. I held the opal close and whispered his name, but he continued to stare off in another direction, before fading completely in sparks of orange.

We came into a realm of very dark clouds broken by greenish brilliance, deep shadows alternating with brightness, as shafts of light broke through and shone down. The water had begun shifting and moving, lifting and dropping the boat uncomfortably.

I heard a stifled cry and, turning, saw a little girl struggling in the water, surfacing and going under again.

"She's drowning!" I cried out to Phee, and as I was about to dive in after her, Phee grabbed my forearm and squeezed it. She shook her head firmly and slowly: *no*.

"But, Phee!" I shrieked. She gave me a look so fierce and certain, I was taken aback.

Another drowning girl appeared on the other side of the boat, and then a crying baby in a wooden creel. Soon we were moving through a sea of wailing babies and little girls shouting, "Help us, please!" Phee remained unmoved, as if she were deaf as well as mute. And I closed my eyes and put my hands over my ears, so that I could muffle the multitude of pleas and obey her. But it went on for what seemed like several unbearable hours.

Gradually, the cries transformed themselves to the screeches of gulls, and the babies and children were all gone.

After that, we found ourselves navigating a narrow lane of water between two islands, where youthful men and women in flowing robes stood on the shores beckoning and calling out to us. Some of them stepped into the tide and came close enough to touch us, offering goblets of wine and pieces of fruit.

A beautiful woman who reminded me of Mam offered me an apple, and on an impulse I extended my arm to receive it. Phee quickly knocked it out of my hand, and as it fell and bobbed on the back of a wave, it became wrinkled and rotted to the core. Phee looked at me fiercely, took out a piece of charcoal and wrote on a wooden plank in the boat's interior: *goblin fruit.*

I looked at the woman who had offered it to me, and right before my eyes her skin withered to yellow, patched with gray. She no longer looked anything like Mam.

We passed those isles, and the sea grew wide again. Still, spectral sheaths of fog undulated and trailed past and alongside us, and I felt afraid.

Phee pointed at the horizon, where the light changed dramatically, and I sensed from her expression that once we got there, we were free of this dangerous realm.

I kept a steady gaze toward the distance, but when I heard a soft scratching at the bottom of the boat, I made the mistake of looking into the water. Girls who looked very much like Breeze and the other ash girls lay on their backs floating about a foot beneath the surface, eyes wide and pleading. The one who looked like Breeze reached her arm up. Even though I knew that it could not really be she, I longed to reach back. She held my eyes, and a sensual thrill rushed through me, a kind of pleasant amnesia so powerful that I began to lean toward her. I wanted to believe in her and the others, and to go with them wherever they took me.

But Phee pulled at me before my finger could touch the apparition's, forcing me fully back into the boat. Irritable and confused at first, I resisted her. But she stood directly before me where I sat and stamped her foot hard, then shook me by the shoulders, with an angry admonishing look.

I returned to my senses, but the scratching and tap-
ping at the bottom of the boat continued, intensifying to
dozens of scratches and taps and frenetic knocks. Phee
held my eyes and squeezed my shoulders, one in each of
her small hands.

"I don't understand this weakness in me, Phee," I said
when I realized what I was doing. "I don't know why I'm
so drawn to them. . . ."

Phee refused to let go, and maintained eye contact
with me, not allowing me to break it.

I was shaking and shining with sweat when our little
boat passed into a new realm of the sea. The light changed
dramatically, the sun streaming over us gold and white,
blinding in flashes as it hit the shifting surfaces of the
water. Squinting, I saw the ships, pale transparent repli-
cas of the Spanish galleons, forming themselves of smoke
and mist, appearing and disappearing and then appearing again. On board, dozens of shades waved from the
decks, the female figureheads leading from the bows, in-
candescent and proud. Before I could remark upon them
to Phee, the cries of swans began to trumpet, a slew of
them circling wildly overhead, feathers floating down
around us. Our boat followed their exuberant lead until
they alighted on an island, transforming into women as
they descended.

Heralding our arrival were birds of various kinds.
Swans, herons and gulls rose on the air, mewing and
screeching, departing and returning. Several of the
women in white and blue-gray waded into the tide to
meet us, their fringed shawls reminiscent of feathered

wings. They brought our boat in and helped us beach it, the sand knee-deep in feathers and down.

Phee disappeared happily into a group of women, while two others led me up a rocky pathway and left me before a white dwelling.

That was when I first saw Danu as she appeared in the doorway. She was perhaps seven feet tall, with large soft limbs, her loose sleeveless gown the color of milk. Though it was sunny, she held a large, lit candelabra, and though the wind was forceful, the flames leaned at extreme angles but did not extinguish.

She began to move slowly toward me, leaving behind faint images of herself after each step, as if she were composed of hundreds of subtler selves that gave her an ever-shifting, translucent aura.

"I am Danu," she said simply in a soft voice that tolled like a bell. Her eyes, glimmering and shot with sunlight, were profoundly clear and steady, like two aquamarine pools. I noticed that she had tiny fine feathers instead of eyelashes and eyebrows.

She hesitated expectantly, and I realized that she was waiting for me to give her the Fire Opal.

I reached into the special pocket of my dress to retrieve it, and as I placed it on her open palm, I watched seven or eight afterimages of her hand as it closed around the opal, sparks of color exploding in the opal's red-orange transparency.

For a few moments, Danu said nothing, just stood there with her head bowed, holding the opal to her heart. In her other hand she held the large, weighty candelabra at a negligent angle, facing away from her. It looked to be made of ornate brass gone greenish at its edges and must have been close to three feet tall.

She sighed, then looked at me, raising her damp eyes.

"Come in," she said quietly.

I followed her along an interior pathway, two lanes of water to either side of us. As we approached a staircase, I was unable to hold back and asked, "Goddess, how can I release my mother and sister from the ice statues on Uria's barge?"

She stopped and turned around, looking at me with gravity, then said reassuringly, "Everything we talk about today, everything you are doing, is in pursuit of that goal, Maeve."

We ascended the stairs, and I followed her out onto a terrace that faced over the sea, where we leaned against a wide white stone railing.·

"The sun is shining brightly today, but you sometimes have days like this on Ard Macha," she said.

"Yes, now and again," I replied.

"Mostly, the weather here matches the weather in Ireland; the rains of the equinox, the damp and mild snows of winter. I try to make this place of my exile as close as possible to the place I have been driven from." She stood very still for a few moments in a concentrated silence, gazing at the sky. Suddenly clouds began to gather and the air darkened. Within moments, it began to pour.

We stepped back under the awning, but she left the candelabra exposed to the rain, which had no effect on the flames.

"Have you taken any time to look really closely at the Fire Opal, Maeve?" she asked.

"In the boat I looked into it and could see someone I miss," I said. I was about to ask her about Francisco, when she began to speak again.

"Yes, it is good for that," she said, and gazed at it. "It is good for many things. It has extraordinary potential and responds to the imagination of the one who holds it."

She held it up in her hands, and it threw deep red and orange reflections onto the white stone of the floor.

"Don't look for anyone in it, Maeve. Just gaze at it and see if any memory is awakened."

As I stared at the Fire Opal, I felt a shadow stirring and remembered a particular day when I was seven, sitting on the stair in the ruins with my mother and the heavy basket of kelp.

"We looked at the horizon," I uttered, in the thrall of the memory. "We felt a kind of yearning."

"That yearning is for a part of yourself that's missing," she said softly as I kept staring into the Fire Opal. "I feel the same longing when I look toward Ireland. We are all exiles, Maeve. I was part human, as you were once part goddess, but we have been separated from ourselves." She studied my face with an anguished sensibility. "I miss the human element," she said, and touched my cheek very softly, as if she were afraid her touch might injure me. "I miss the perpetual uncertainties, the constant searching and getting lost in wishes and desires. Being a goddess can be isolating, and even static. Without human contact, the element of drama is lost."

"I was once part goddess?" I asked.

"All the women of Ard Macha were. Do you sense, under the surface, the great potential that is hidden from you? It is like you own a treasure chest but you have lost the key. That day when you were seven, when you and your mother sat on the stair in the ruins with the basket of kelp, something significant happened. Do you remember?"

I looked at her helplessly, not knowing the answer.

"Look again at the Fire Opal." She held it cupped in her hand to block some of the light from the sky. A vague shadow moved within the opal, and I had the feeling that something inside it was looking at me. It came closer, and with a pulse of shock, I recognized the face of the Answerer, the broken sword, which I had hidden from my brothers so many years ago.

"I found it in the kelp that day," I said, and began to shiver. "It had come up on a big wave. For some reason, until now I had forgotten about it."

"I want to tell you about the significance of the Answerer," she said.

I followed her off the porch and back into the room, where she set the Fire Opal on a stand that seemed made especially for it. Very slowly the stand began to revolve, and the Fire Opal picked up all the light in the nearly empty room and any light coming in from outside, casting bright refractions onto the bare white walls.

Danu took my shawl gently from my shoulders and smiled, acknowledging its similarity to her own. She drew out a threaded needle and a handful of very tiny red beads. As she continued to speak, she slowly sewed the tiny beads into various places on my shawl.

"Almost seven centuries ago, I still ruled Ard Macha. As long as the last primeval forest grew there, it sent its fertilizing sparks on the wind currents, which traveled slowly around the world, and because the forest existed at all," she said, and leaned into me, emphasizing the words, *"the world's potential was still full of texture. There was sound in silence. There was luminosity in darkness."*

As Danu spoke, I saw, as if from above, a thick forest of formidable trees spanning hills and a deep valley. I seemed to be moving on the air above them in a westerly direction until I reached the sea. The trees nearest the beach strained and leaned inland, stunted by the Atlantic gales.

And there were the ruins, before they were ruins: pristine towers and walls, arches and pediments. The tumultuous Atlantic crashed and rolled, foaming up a vast staircase and slapping at the massive doors.

Suddenly I was inside the edifice, moving through a corridor until I entered a chamber, a kind of apothecary filled with bottles and plants. On one of the walls hung charts and diagrams of the cross sections of flowers and their buds. That's when I saw the red jewel stars embedded in the green and gray marble of the wall, and recognized this chamber as the collapsed room where I would one day, as a child of seven, hide the Answerer.

In the center of the room, a group of young women wearing sleeveless crimson gowns and gold torc bracelets on their bare upper arms were chanting softly, and moving slowly around a kind of altar. I recognized the chant as the same language the Swan Woman had lapsed into when she'd given me the bottles.

Suddenly I was not just a spectator, but one of the chanting women. We were focused on the Fire Opal, displayed there on a stand, similar to the one Danu had. One young woman seemed to be leading everything. She wore a kind of garland of small lit candles on her head. She held her arms up in a gesture, and we all responded with an introspective silence.

"My priestesses," Danu said, narrating in the background, *"were the keepers of the Fire Opal."*

Our leader approached the Fire Opal ceremonially and took it in her hands, placing it carefully into a glass box with brass hinges. Removing a large ring of keys from the belt around her waist, she selected one and locked the box, then placed it on a shelf behind a dark velvet curtain. She rang a small bell, and we all formed a single file line and followed her out of the room along a narrow hallway with very high ceilings. Through the tall windows above us, all manner of birds flew in and out, their chirping and singing echoing loudly. Even herons swept past us, some on foot, some flying horizontally, low to the ground.

We arrived at a large entrance hall, where Danu awaited us.

"I told my priestesses that we would be entertaining the goddess Uria and her handmaidens."

Looking through a wide arch, I saw a very large woman in armor crafted of black iron, the chest and back piece recognizable to me as the one Tom Cavan would one day dig out of the bog. She was sitting among a congregation of women in dark gray who hunched together, some peering over their shoulders at us with cool, suspicious eyes.

"I did not know everything I should have known about her at the time," Danu said. "Word had not yet spread across Ireland about her true nature. I knew only that she had evolved into goddess status, having distinguished herself as a warrior queen. I believed her when she said she had come posing no threat to us, only needing a place to rest and to prepare her ship before leaving Ireland for the northern Greenland waters. She had asked to stay for three days.

"I would find out when it was too late that she had come as a Valkyrie, a corpse goddess, from the land of the Vikings. While the Irish had been celebrating victory after the definitive battle against the invading Vikings at Clontarf, Uria, uninjured, had stolen the ancient weapon from Brian Boru, the great Irish hero. It was the weapon I had bestowed upon him myself, made by druidesses, the metal and stone that composes it taken from the sacred spring of boiling minerals. The druidesses named it the Answerer, and presented it to me, and I in turn presented it to Brian Boru, the greatest protector of Ireland. He called it his battle-axe, although, as you know, it looks nothing like an axe at all."

I followed the priestesses to help them bring out platters of fish and fruit for Uria and her women.

As I set down a pitcher of wine, one of these women grabbed my forearm with clawed fingers and, peering at me with pale, amber eyes, said, "We expect to eat roast bird, preferably heron or pelican."

Another priestess near me who overheard this turned and said, "Birds are holy to Danu and are never eaten in her house."

The women laughed, rolling their eyes, some speaking in ironic tones to one another under their breath. One of these women got up and whispered directly into Uria's ear.

Feathers littered these rooms and halls, and one happened to be on the table where Uria sat. She lifted her fork high, then in a grand and violent gesture, jabbed the feather and waved it back and forth on the air before she ate it.

There was another shift in time. I found myself walking quietly into a dim corridor, surrounded by more of Danu's priestesses, when we came upon a gang of Uria's women crouched around several dead birds, eating them, blood and feathers all over their hands and faces. The other priestesses I was with rushed forward, confronting them. A fight broke out, but I was behind the others, being jostled, not privy to what was going on at the front of the scuffle.

I heard a loud jingling of keys, but the commotion was so rough in that narrow area, I was pushed brutally aside, the air knocked out of me. More tumult ensued and footsteps rushed past. My head ached so badly I couldn't move. When I finally lifted myself up on one arm, I saw Danu's head priestess, the keeper of the keys, lying in a heap, beaten and bloodied on the stone floor, the flames mostly all gone out on the garland on her head.

I crept over to her and touched her shoulder. She was cold. The keys had been torn from her belt. I listened at her chest, but there was no heartbeat.

Time blurred and shifted again.

I found myself on the great stairs before Danu's palace, among the priestesses. Danu appeared from within the nearby forest, stepping out onto a clearing. The white of her gown emitted wisps of ethereal light, like mist rising from damp water. She stood firmly, her legs wide, and leaned slightly forward. Ready for battle, she emitted high-pitched vibrations like dozens of shivering tuning forks. Each time she moved, turning her head or lifting her arm, faint trailers of herself appeared momentarily and dissolved.

Uria came from around a tower wall, grown double her height, flesh, hair and her armor painted silver for battle. The muscles at Uria's neck strained, and her jaw ground against itself. When she opened her mouth, foam flew from her lips. She pointed her weapon at Danu, and I recognized the Answerer, although the sword was completely intact and the one-eyed face on the handle wore an expression of horror.

Uria seemed to ignite from within like a human lantern, and the fire that came from her body channeled itself through the handle of the Answerer and flew at Danu like a bolt of lightning.

But Danu moved quickly, and the bolt hit a great oak tree behind her, setting it aflame.

Uria aimed again for Danu, but this time the weapon itself seemed to convulse, and catapulted from her hand as if of its own will. The sword pierced the thick trunk of another oak. Several of Uria's henchwomen rushed the tree, burning themselves in the blazes of the giant oak beside it as they struggled to pull the Answerer free. But the sword was so deeply buried in the bark that it snapped off with their efforts. Uria's henchwomen dropped it in the blaze surrounding the burning oak, too injured to retrieve it. Then Danu grabbed it and hurled it into the darkness of the forest.

Uria crouched, cinders and smoke issuing from her eyes and ears.

"That is when I understood how badly Uria needed that weapon. Without it to channel this eerie fire that generated directly from her own body, she was engulfed and scorched by it, in danger of self-immolation."

Uria ran toward the ocean and toppled down in the tide, vast issues of hissing steam rising from her. After a few minutes the steam died down, but she seemed unable to rise, needing the water to keep washing over her.

Danu advised us, her priestesses, to stay back and not to take any action.

Uria's henchwomen guarded their goddess fiercely, some of them shape-shifting into vultures, flying threateningly in circles.

"Go!" Uria's head had risen out of the tide. "Into the woods. Bring the weapon!" she ordered in a booming bass voice.

"But, Goddess, it is broken," one of the women said.

Uria rose onto one muscular arm, shaking with effort. "Bring it to me!" she called, and the fire under the surface lit her face and neck so it shone a blinding white, threatening again to break into flame. In an agony, she submerged herself again.

Time blurred and shifted again, and now I seemed to be watching everything from the air. The forest burned in bright torrents, smoke rising.

"You see, Uria knew that the handle is where the power resides in that weapon. The blade itself is nothing special and can be easily replaced. But the ice-cold marble and the unique mineral composition of the handle had a way of conducting the fire of her nature through her and away from her so that she could use it against others. Without the Answerer, Uria is helpless and will burn in her own rage. And that is why she preserves herself in the cocoon of ice."

I could no longer see Ard Macha below. I was back in the little room with Danu. She grasped the Fire Opal in her hand, and all imagery on the walls disappeared.

"At that point, we didn't know the attack on the birds and the murder of the head priestess were all distractions to cause a confrontation. Uria's henchwomen had broken into the altar and had taken the Fire Opal.

"The primeval forest, the last of its kind, was destroyed. That fire could not be put out, and the Fire Opal is the only seed with the power to replant it. Uria's goal has been to make nature less than it is meant to be. Over time, people have forgotten their natural sovereignty, their intimate ties to the elements. She has managed to keep the opal from me for this long. I have it again, but we are not finished.

"Some of the elementals that lived in the woods died in the flames, while others fled, some by air, some by sea. When she managed, in her weakness, to get back to her ship, Uria had my Fire Opal. But she needed the Answerer as well. A slew of screeching vulture women flew into the smoky woods as the fires died down, pulling burned oaks up by their roots and tossing them high and far in long arcs to the sea.

"My priestesses found the weapon first, and I hid it carefully in a secret vault in the sea, in a place that even Uria's mermaids would never find, no matter how well they trolled the waters.

"But the world was in chaos after that battle. Uria's vulture women were a constant threat, hounding me and murdering my priestesses, searching tirelessly in the burnt ruins of the forest for the battle-axe. I was forced to exile myself from Ireland. And after Uria sailed in her Viking ship back to some arctic land, I heard that she had to move through an emanation and in a tightly controlled environment if she meant to survive.

"At seven years old, Maeve, you came into contact

with the broken battle-axe, the Answerer. You responded to it with pure instinct. It is an object, yet it is also sentient, as you immediately understood."

"I didn't feel evil coming from it," I said.

"It isn't evil. It was never meant for such ill usage as Uria put it to. You must remember that. It was originally the staff and weapon of the great Brian Boru. It's good that you forgot it, too, Maeve. Forgotten, it has been safest. It is because you buried it where light could attach itself to it again that Ishleen came. Ishleen is the Swan Daughter, come to herald the return of the elementals to Ard Macha. When Tom Cavan unearthed the armor, the poisonous threat he unleashed killed the delicate Ishleen in her first incarnation. But your mother, in her powerfully instinctive way, knew and yearned for her dead child's return, though she was thought to be mad.

"The night your mother gave birth again to Ishleen, Uria's henchwoman came to take her, but your mother had given you the charm necklace to wear while you held Ishleen. You had gone a step further and put the necklace on Ishleen. Uria's henchwoman could not take her because of it, and took your mother's ghost soul instead, thinking that the baby would have a poor chance of survival. Because you've insisted Ishleen always wear the chain, they were not able to get her for years.

"What they really hound that area for is the Answerer, but they cannot sense its location there because it does not smell of the poison of Uria. It has undergone intense purification in the room that was once the priestesses' apothecary. For now, it must remain just where it is. It is

246

extremely unlikely that they could ever find it in that sacred place.

"As I've said, Maeve, this Fire Opal, which you have brought me at great risk to yourself, is the seed upon which the entire world might turn."

She tied the last bit of thread, then held the shawl up in the light. The rain stopped and the clouds cleared. In the sunlight, the shawl glistened as if with red embers.

"Your shawl is inundated with little beads of potential fire. If you are faced with the threat of Uria, breathe hot breath onto this shawl and you will ignite in an aura of flame, flames in which you will be completely safe."

"Goddess, how do I release my mother and sister and all the tundra women from the ice?" I pleaded.

She nodded and went on. "The five tundra woman priestesses, who went on Uria's barge and were eventually killed, had brought a druid wheel with a triple spiral emblem forged on it. It was meant to set life and time back into true motion, to change the regressive lack of life force, the suspension from life that holds the icy air around Uria. Probably rusted or buried in ice, the wheel was likely discovered by one of the henchwomen and turned tight in the opposite direction. No growth, no transformation can occur as long as the wheel is stuck so tightly, only a long icy purgatory of waiting. That atmosphere is also maintained by lack of true fire; the false light drains vitality and holds life in abeyance. Uria is too terrified to move much at all. The reintroduction of true fire onto that barge, no matter how secretly those fires are being burned, has likely already begun to make changes in the atmosphere, and because of the presence of fire, it is likely that the wheel, if you can find it, will be easier to turn and release. Life will inevitably rush in."

"Will it work, what the tundra girls have planned? Can the ghost souls of our mothers go back into their bodies?"

"It is possible for the ghost souls to return to the bodies, but you must realize that by having been separated that way, they are changed. A thread has been broken. If they return to their bodies, they might not cleave to them the way they once did. They will inhabit them mostly, but they might drift loose sometimes, especially at night during sleep. It's important that the ethereal dresses always be kept nearby to contain them and give them form. The tundra girls are very right about the dangers. Ghost souls dissolve or break into particles in a rough wind. Their minds go back into the mind of nature herself, and particles also go into the minds and souls and bodies of their children and loved ones, but it is a kind of death. It is a separation."

I sighed and closed my eyes. Everything before me felt daunting, and I realized that my neck and back were aching. Exhausted, I rubbed my eyes and heard my stomach rumble. But I knew I could not let myself give in to this desire for rest.

I opened my eyes and found Danu leaning slightly toward me, studying my face with soft intensity. She reached out, her hand hovering near the side of my cheek, hesitating to touch.

"How I miss the human element," she said quietly, almost apologetically. "Seven centuries is a very long time. Memory grows weaker and weaker. We are all in danger of losing touch with our true histories.

"You are tired, Maeve. Unfortunately, there is too little time. You must get back before the narcotic effect wears off." She stood and, taking my hand, led me back out through the dwelling, and down the stairs. Something occurred to her, and she stopped in the middle of a corridor. "Remember, Uria has been using Tom Cavan as a human agent, but she doesn't trust him. And I doubt that he trusts her. Plus, he is ambitious, which frightens her, but until she has the Answerer, she is dependent upon him. I imagine that he is after it himself. If the opportunity ever arises and he asks if you know where it is, you should suggest to him that it is in a bog south of Ard Macha near the hill at Rosscoyne. The peat there is intensely absorbent, the most entrapping in Ireland. Creatures and things unlucky enough to fall in rarely find their way out without help. It is not turf he can cut with so much ease as the bogs of Ard Macha. And it is filled with all manner of sunken objects. It will keep him endlessly busy, if he doesn't tumble in himself."

She took two pieces of beige silk from a pocket in her gown. They floated, suspending themselves on the air before her. She concentrated on them, and images appeared on the surfaces as if drawn. "Here are two maps of the Rosscoyne bog," she said. "Possession of these can make the lie seem more believable.

"In any case, Maeve, pit Uria and Tom Cavan against each other. And remember that Uria's rage weakens her without the Answerer."

We passed a dining hall where Phee and a group of Swan Women were sitting around a massive table laid with breads and cheeses, fruit and cake, eating and talking softly.

"Goddess," I said to Danu, pointing in at the feast, my stomach grumbling.

"I'm sorry, Maeve, but you cannot eat the food of the Other World. You have too much business left in Ireland."

"But I feel weak, Goddess," I said.

"You must find the strength within yourself, Maeve," she answered.

Seeing me looking in, Phee raced out and embraced me. I kissed her on the crown of her head. She made numerous excited signs to me, which I was too hungry and distracted to try to decipher. She pointed at someone—a pale, enigmatic-looking woman who was gazing in another direction, as if lost in thought. I wondered if this was some incarnation of Phee's mother, but before I could ask, Danu swept me off and out the door.

When we reached the beach where my little boat waited, Danu said, "You know that if all goes well, I will see you again. There will be something more I will want you to do."

She took both my hands and pressed them to her belly pocket, where the Fire Opal was. Warm pleasant sparks moved in currents through my hands. She bent down and kissed my forehead.

I boarded my vessel, and she told me to be careful since I was now traveling alone.

"You know not to be enticed by anything or to eat anything as long as you are in the waters of the Shee. Leaving is always less threatening than trying to get here, but it is possible that something still might happen."

"Nothing will distract me, Goddess. I will think of my mother and sister."

It occurred to me as the boat headed eastward that I had never asked her about Francisco. I felt a sudden painful remorse at this omission. Maybe, I thought, I had not asked on purpose, afraid of the answer she might have had for me.

I looked at her watching from the shore. She held both hands pressed against the Fire Opal in her belly pocket.

Soon she was very far away, and when I could no longer see her island at all, I felt frightened of the wide ocean before me.

The air grew humid and the sky overcast, dim clouds grumbling and flashing as if it were about to pour again. An intense almost green darkness fell over the horizon around me. I shivered and sat curled into myself as the boat lifted and fell on the waves.

CHAPTER 21

As I sailed eastward, the sky grew even dimmer and heavier. I felt uncomfortably hungry and was so unable to focus clearly that I tried to distract myself with other thoughts: the image of swans transforming into women, of words that the goddess had spoken to me. I relived again and again everything I had witnessed in the Ard Macha of seven centuries past, but that had the effect of exhausting me. So I gave myself over to comforting memories of Francisco. I remembered the soft light coming into Mam's face as he'd called her "Señora" and touched the triple spiral, causing it to hum. And I thought of the night I'd sat with him in the sand under the figurehead of *Nuestra Señora de la Soledad,* and he'd put his arms around me.

These thoughts warmed me until I saw an island far up

ahead to the left with the sun shining over it. A tree with large orange fruits grew on the beach. The wind blew almost violently, propelling my boat closer, but still everything was soundless but my own breathing.

The boat arrived at the island and beached itself in the slender margin of sand past the tide. I got out, shaking with hunger, approached the tree and pulled one of the oranges down.

I sank my teeth into it, tearing away the rind and eating the juicy pulp, consuming it in a kind of frenzy, juice dripping over my chin and hands.

I had finished and was considering taking another when I saw a figure moving farther inland, a man who could have been Francisco, his hair and oat-colored shirt rippling in the strong, silent gusts. He was waiting there in the distance, expectantly looking off in another direction. I waved wildly and tried to scream his name, but I had no voice.

Remaining oblivious of my presence, he began to walk inland, away from me.

Suddenly there was sound again, soft breezes and the rush of the tide. I ran in the direction the man had gone. The sun got brighter, transforming everything, so I had to shield my eyes with my hands.

Ahead were more trees like the one on the beach, thick with deep green leaves and heavy with oranges. Others, less ornate, were clustered with pale brown nuts.

My skin gloried in the warm, clear air and the smell of citrus and roses. Something very subtle but intoxicating mixed itself with the other fragrances, a vague earthy smell that caused my blood to race.

The second time it rushed me, I knew with a shock what it was: the scent of Francisco's skin and hair, blown to me on the back of a breeze. In the far distance, I saw him pass between two orange trees. Now I had no doubts. It was Francisco. I ran breathlessly after him, but when I reached the sunny clearing where I'd seen him go, he was nowhere around.

A peacock strutted past, and I followed it. I found myself before a large house, the sun making the plain white walls so bright that I had to squint. There were tall open arches and curtains blowing lightly outward in the soft breezes.

At the entrance of the house, roses grew in abundance. The view of the sea from here was nothing like the dim Atlantic at the northwest of Ireland or the clouded seas I had been traveling on. This sea was drenched in sunlight and shimmered like thousands of silver coins.

As I was about to go into the archway of the house, I saw a name engraved in majestic stone above the lintel: FRANCISCO CORTEZ.

My heart raced. I passed from the brilliant sunlight outside into the shade of the partial interior, shafts of brightness breaking the dark here and there, slanting through the arches. Something moved in my peripheral vision and I gasped, "Francisco!" But it was just the work of a ghostly curtain rippling and casting shadows on the wall.

Small green fruits and bright red chilies hung from little potted trees along the floor. I ascended a white stone staircase toward the upper house and was startled again, but this time by a tall, dark wood cabinet facing me like a confronting presence. I touched it. "Francisco," I said, as if he might emerge from the wood.

Other pieces of furniture like it stood at various places and at different angles in the room, and I passed through feeling an excited chill, as if they were watching me. I went down a hallway of closed wooden doors and ascended another set of stairs to the highest and dimmest floor. Looking out the open arch, I saw that dusk had suddenly gathered, as if time had passed rapidly.

It was then, as I gazed down to the yard below, that I had the sense that there was something urgent I was supposed to be doing, but I could not recall what it was. It pulled at me as I stared at the night-blooming flowers beginning to open their white trumpets to the moon.

"What is it?" I asked myself, half deliriously. But whatever it was seemed to have detached itself from details and memory. The sweetness of the air, its clarity and coolness, relaxed and intoxicated me. The heads of the flowers trembled on their long slender necks. I could not concentrate on anything but the proximity of Francisco.

The dim reverberating tinkle of a bell sounded from within the house. "Francisco," I whispered, and closed my eyes. "Where are you?"

A moment later I sensed him there, and smelled him on a gush of air. I remained very still, my attention finely tuned to the atmosphere, every sound, every slight change in temperature and fragrance. I took in my breath. This game served only to intensify the ache I felt to see him and eclipsed the other sense that there was somewhere I needed to go and something I needed to remember.

As I roamed the deepening shadows of the rooms, the wind blew, and doors creaked and slammed downstairs. Instead of frightening me, this excited me.

He was hiding, but I would hide, too. We were playing an exhilarating game, the feeling of expectation invigorating to the point of distraction.

I opened the door to a room and saw dozens of flickering candles burning and pulsing before shrines to unknown female saints, some wearing thorny roses and ruffled mantles sewn with silver thread, all romantic-looking with dark eyes and red glistening lips. One of them, who looked like the figurehead on *La Hermana de la Luna,* turned her head slowly toward me and blinked her eyes. It did not seem strange that the statues in this place moved. She nodded, and I nodded back, and for a moment I felt it again, that uneasy urgency that I had something important to do. But I dismissed it when, from my peripheral vision, I saw movement and a flash of light near the stairwell. I hid in a recess behind the door, holding my breath, certain it was him at last. When I could bear it no longer, I jumped out. Instead of Francisco, I discovered an image of myself in a long mirror. Yet I did not really feel that the figure was me. She wore an extraordinary jewel-encrusted dress, more ornate than any I had ever seen. She smiled playfully, moving forward, and suddenly the mirror was gone. She tilted her head, little wheels of light turning in her eyes, a palpable physical presence, breathing near me. She stifled a laugh as if I amused her.

"Go on," she urged. "Keep looking for him."

I felt a vague revulsion and unease. I reached out to touch her, but my fingers found a flat, cool surface. The mirror was there again, and the self looking back at me was just me, weathered by my journey, my pupils very large and shining as if I were suffering with fever, dusky circles beneath my eyes. My hair was intensely wind-matted, and I could see my chest rising and falling very hard as I breathed.

Shaken, I rushed away and told myself it had only been a hallucination caused by my exhaustion. My desire to see Francisco was so strong, my heart palpitated. I went down to the second floor and began listening at each door, until I heard breathing. All my pulses raced. I threw the door open.

My stomach fell like a lead weight. She was there again in her shimmering multifaceted dress. A smile crept across her face, and her eyes went wide. She was looking at something over my shoulder behind me. She pointed. "There he is!" she whispered.

I gasped as I turned. Francisco was there, an arm's length away from me, his fragrant proximity warming the air between us. He grasped my hands and broke into a full smile, the two masculine dimples deepening, the ruby shining between his white teeth.

But it was the depth of his eyes, dark and flecked with

amber, that made me sure of him—sure that this was no flight of fancy, no illusion. Danu's warnings came vaguely to mind. But who she was to me, and why she had warned me, had become unclear. No, whatever I had tried so hard to remember earlier was gone, leaving only the residue of a lost dream. Strangely, it didn't matter that the rooms shifted and that things around us moved or disappeared. In every tingling fiber of my body, I knew that Francisco, at least, was real. "Maeve, Maeve," he whispered, then embraced me and sighed; I felt then that he had been longing for me as much as I had for him.

He touched the side of my face and my hair, as if it were he who needed reassurance that I was real.

I heard soft laughter behind me and, looking back, saw the reflection watching us with fascinated eyes. Francisco seemed unperturbed by her presence.

"Let's leave here, Francisco," I pleaded.

No sooner had I said it than we found ourselves outside at a gypsy camp where men and women danced around a fire in the moonlight. A man sang, a melodious howl to the moon, and the others whistled and hooted and clapped, and two women danced, one shaking a tambourine, the other playing tinkling finger cymbals. The night sky was vivid blue and filled with stars, so many of them shooting it was like fireworks, leaving streaks and threads of light on the sky.

The sea roared and the moon slid across the heavens. A group of stars fell into the sea all at once and caused an explosion of light, and those particles flew and floated everywhere, like lit cinders from a fire.

Francisco made a necklace of night-blooming flowers for me by weaving their green fronds together. Slow, pleasurable shudders moved over the surface of my skin as he hung it around my neck.

Time seemed to contract and stretch, clouds sometimes rampaging over the sea, rapid ebbs of passing days and nights while we remained on the periphery of the gypsy camp dancing or entangled in each other's arms. The necklace of flowers stayed alive, breathing at my ear, sighing sometimes, closing at daylight, opening again at dark as full-throated as trumpets.

Early one morning, I awakened to the sound of a harp, swirling scales of music ascending and descending. At first, the music gave intense pleasure, but it soon began reawakening the nagging urgency, the sense that I had forgotten something. In waves of anxiety, accompanied by the shiver of harp strings, I struggled to remember. But my concentration was broken when Francisco pointed to a figure approaching from a distance. It was a priest in a long brown robe with a belt of rope tied around his waist and a large, heavy crucifix hanging around his neck. He married Francisco and me, blessing us with the sign of the cross, then kissing us each on the forehead. The gypsies cried out in celebration, then led us to a secluded beach where, hidden behind an embankment of rock, we found a bed with an iron frame, the sea rushing around its legs.

We lay down side by side and embraced as the others receded and left us to ourselves. At some point, the tide carried the bed into the water. We lay facing each other, the bed gently rocking on the waves like a boat.

We slept. I'd awaken for brief periods to the sound of the sea, or the sensation of Francisco's lips pressed at my temple. But then a moment occurred when I heard the music coming again from somewhere nearby. I listened, hardly breathing as the harp transformed into voices. I suddenly recognized "The Canticle of Fire," though I did not know the name of it or where I had heard it before. I knew only that I had heard it and that it was related to the confused urgency that haunted me. My eyes dampened and an unnameable yearning filled me. It was all there very close, like shadows behind a curtain. I ached to see everything clearly.

Francisco was sound asleep. The tide had gone out, and the bed stood again in the sand, having sailed and beached itself in front of the house with Francisco's name above the lintel. On the departing tide, I saw my shawl, the tiny red jewels glistening, while on the nearby shore a group of gypsies stared at it covetously, intent upon it; two of the women began to wade in toward it. I dove into the water, and before they could get the shawl, I retrieved it and swam back to shore and to the bed, where Francisco still lay.

Everything felt ominously wrong. I stared at Francisco, and saw with horror that with each exhalation, he grew transparent, partially invisible; with each inhalation, he took solid form again. My heart raced with panic, and "The Canticle of Fire," which had remained softly playing on the air the entire time, grew in volume. The closer I looked at him, the stranger he appeared: his smooth forehead now furrowed, and his full lips were thin and tense and squeezed at the corners.

One of the night-blooming flowers on the necklace, which was wound around the iron curlicues of the bedpost, began to whisper, "He isn't real. He isn't real."

His eyes, when he opened them, were not brown but a dull, pale green, the whites a wash of pink. Perhaps it was my astonishment that kept me staring into his face, or maybe it was a wish that this not be true, but as I did, gray fur began growing over his skin, and his ears became long and pointed. As I backed away, the bed disappeared and he began to dissolve, leaving only an outline in the sand.

I heard a crackling sound and looked toward the house, where the curtains were on fire, and soon the walls were ignited. The orange trees in front shimmered blue at their edges, staggering like men before they fell. Instead of Francisco's name above the lintel, I saw my own name carved there: MAEVE O'TULLAGH. And beneath it, looking out the open door, stood the reflection that looked like me wearing the heavy jewel-encrusted dress. She gave a wistful smile, unperturbed by the flames that were now engulfing her. The jewels on her dress popped and snapped in the heat, some flying off in arcs. The letters of my name glowed deep orange in the flames above her, and soon the entire structure collapsed over her in a rage of fire. And far more quickly than if any of it had been real, the house was gone in a gust of black smoke.

Tortured by an awful confusion, I knelt down and touched the sandy outline of the man I had thought was Francisco. A tide rushed in and washed it fully away.

Everything changed suddenly. The trees disappeared. It was a dead island, nothing but dry dust and stone.

On the vacant shore, gilded by the lowering sun, I saw Danu watching me, waiting. On the sand beside her stood her large, ornately wrought candelabra. It held three burning candles, the flames leaning and rippling in the wind. As I approached, dusk deepened around us, great banks of dimming cloud rearing and dissolving.

Mam and Ishleen flashed through my thoughts, and I was gripped with panic. I remembered the black iron boxes and the urgency that I return before the narcotic wore off. Overcome with remorse and dread, I began to run toward the goddess.

"How long have I been here?" I cried out.

"Three days," she answered calmly.

"I thought it was longer."

"Time is distorted here in the Realm of the Shee. You ate the goblin fruit."

"I was hungry, and I thought I had already left the waters of the Shee."

Danu shook her head. "I have been here on this beach almost the entire time waiting for you. But you were in the thrall of your dream. Even I could not have brought you back, and I worried that you might not return at all."

"It was real, Goddess," I said, and began to weep. "He was real."

She looked at me sadly and shook her head. "No."

"Where is he, Goddess?" I asked. "Is Francisco still alive?"

"He may be alive, but if he is, he has undergone some great transformation."

"What do you mean?"

"Sometimes people don't die in the usual way. They transform. But there's no time now to speak about that. Because you long so much for Francisco, you are too vulnerable to the illusions of the Shee. Take this with you." She pointed to the candelabra. "These flames will never go out, and the light they issue will help you distinguish between what is real and what is illusion."

"Have I ruined everything?" I asked.

"The plan will not be so seamless now, Maeve. They'll know that you've been gone when you return. Just remember everything I've told you."

"Where is my boat?"

"It's drifted off, or it's traveled back without you." She pointed seaward, and to the west I saw the faint ghost of *Nuestra Señora de la Soledad* drifting at anchor. "Grasp the candelabra," she instructed. "It will take you."

I reached down and took hold of the heavy yoke below the burning candles.

"Kick the hem of the dress softly and deliberately," she said.

I obeyed her, and the dress lifted me into the air. She watched me gravely from below as I sailed toward the ghost ship.

* * *

The dark green skies gathered again as we moved through the Realm of the Shee. The ghosts of Francisco's former crew members listened as I struggled to come to terms with what I'd experienced.

"I was sure it was Francisco," I said. "It seemed like him the entire time, until the very end."

They nodded with compassion and spoke gently to me in Spanish.

"*Sabemos, niña.*"

"*No te preocupes.*"

"*Todo va estar bien, niña querida.*"

And though I did not understand every consolation they muttered, I tried to take comfort.

CHAPTER 22

I knew we were close to the barge when I saw the wall of mist ahead. To my surprise, *Mananan's Vessel* was there rocking on the waves. I waved goodbye to the Spanish ghosts and, carrying the candelabra, leaned into the open air. The dress, swelling with wind, lifted and carried me down toward the little boat. Struggling to steady myself as I stepped into it, I dropped the candelabra and it fell into the sea.

I looked over the side and saw it sinking deeper and deeper, turning gracefully as it did, flames still alight.

Just at that moment, coming from the direction of the barge, a boat penetrated the mist. Standing at its center was Tom Cavan, an awful composure about him, his face strange and heavy, not a muscle stirring.

I stood up with shock and realized that he was another

two or three inches taller. He wore a new coat of rich crimson velvet, embroidered with gold thread and pearls. His hair had grown even longer and hung in thick lion-colored waves near his shoulders.

The entire world went quiet as his boat reached mine, bumping into its stern. My backbone froze as he towered over me.

"Where did you go?" he asked.

I remembered Danu's words that I should play on the mistrust between Uria and Tom. "I am not supposed to tell you. . . ."

The silence intensified. The wind hummed as it blew his hair.

"Tell me."

"I have been on an errand."

"An errand for whom?"

When I remained silent, his eyes narrowed.

"For Uria," I said, "but I promised not to reveal what it was about."

He stared at me.

With a sudden impulsiveness, I said, "I'll tell you everything if you release my mother and sister from the ice."

He focused on me with a sardonic expression, the wind still blowing his hair. "They aren't in the ice any longer."

My head rang. I wanted to speak, but I could not find the words.

"I told you that if you betrayed me in any way, I would enclose them in darkness, and that's what I've done. They are in the iron boxes."

Nausea rose in my stomach. "I won't tell you what I know unless you release them and let them go back to their bodies at Ard Macha."

"No, Maeve O'Tullagh. You don't set the conditions for anything here. Tell me everything and I won't drop the boxes into the sea, where they'd likely never be found."

"Uria wanted me to find out the location of something," I blurted out.

"Of what?" he demanded.

"A certain"—I paused for effect—"weapon."

A muscle on his upper lip contracted. "And did you find out where it is?"

I did not answer but touched my pocket, pretending to check on something.

"What do you have there?" he demanded.

I hesitated.

"Give it to me."

I tried to appear as reluctant as possible as I took out one of Danu's maps drawn on the hardened silk, the location of the bog near Rosscoyne highlighted with gold thread.

He took it roughly.

"Where did you get this?"

"A servant of the goddess Danu gave it to me. A Swan Woman whom I met in the waters of the Shee."

"This is a bog, south of Ard Macha," he said, studying it. "Near Rosscoyne."

The wall of mist behind him exuded humidity like soft white smoke. He froze a moment, his eyes searching mine, then asked, "Why would she give you that information?"

My mind raced for an answer. "Because she wants me to get it myself and bring it back to Danu."

"I have heard that the weapon cannot pass through the Realm of the Shee into the Other World."

"Seven centuries have passed. Now it can be brought to the Holy Isles," I said.

He looked at me skeptically, our two boats rocking on the uneven waves. "Why do you tell me all this so willingly?"

I knew I should have held back longer to make my lie more convincing, but my unease over Mam and Ishleen made me desperate. "I want you to release my mother and sister."

This was true, but it also seemed to satisfy him in regard to my carelessly executed lie. As he studied the map further, I could not hold myself back from crying out, "Please take them out of the boxes!"

A little smile lit his deadened features, and I saw a flash of the boyhood Tom Cavan. "If I find the weapon with the help of the map, then I will release them. I'll even send them back to Ard Macha, but *only* if I find the weapon here."

He took a step closer, towering over me. Taking note of my confused expression, he puffed up his chest and said, "Do you know, Maeve, how a man becomes a god? By refusing to be bound by human limitation. I have learned a great deal from Uria. When you hear her heartbeat at the core of this barge, you must understand that it is pure obsession that drives her, an ancient grudge she keeps against the goddess Danu. Everything here, this entire barge, is driven by that obsession.

"But we are at the dawn of a new age, and new gods will reign." He looked at the map. "It is good that you've given me this. Still, you and I have a long way to go."

I remained nervously silent. I felt his attention on me soften, and averted my eyes.

"This palace . . . this barge," he said, pointing into the mist, "would not be such a bad place to spend eternity, would it?"

"It's too cold," I said.

"There's plenty of blue fire."

"That doesn't make anyone warm."

"It's very strong in some situations. You saw the burns on those little girls' arms and hands."

"Those are ice burns," I said. "Anyone living here is on the verge of freezing all the time."

"You can grow accustomed to it. I have. I have learned to experience the warmth of the fire."

"It is only the illusion of warmth," I said. "It isn't real."

"Maybe the illusion is enough, Maeve," he said with a softly challenging expression.

"No," I said plainly.

He looked annoyed, and was about to say something else when another boat appeared through the mist, three of Uria's "ladies" in their human forms standing on deck.

"They are coming with me," Tom said. "They are turning their allegiance over to me because they understand that we are at the dawn of a new age. They know how weak Uria is. All of them will eventually be loyal to me."

I noticed that some of the misbegotten mermaids were circling near the surface around his boat, peering up worshipfully at him through the water. A few suddenly hoisted themselves into the air, making whimpering noises.

"They are with me, too. The truth is, all of them are ready, as soon as power changes hands, to come to my side."

Mrs. Cavan appeared on her own small boat immediately after the vulture women. Tom addressed her sternly. "Make sure Maeve does not get away. I'll be back in a day or so, I hope." He turned and looked at me as one of the vulture women tied my hands behind my back. "If you see Uria, you will tell her nothing. Do you understand? Nothing about the things you've shared with me. If you do, the two iron boxes will be dropped into the sea." His eyes sparkled. "Our wedding will go on as planned, after I've found what I'm looking for."

At this, the mermaids grew distressed and swam in sputtering, frantic circles beneath my boat, causing it to rock so that I thought I'd fall in.

"Stop!" Tom yelled.

So admonished, they retreated into the depths, and the water went still.

Looking both amused and proud, Tom glanced expectantly at me to see if I was impressed, but I refused to offer any sign that I was.

"I'm sure that you will behave from now on, but if it is the case that I must always hold something over your head, Maeve O'Tullagh, so be it. Even when we are married to each other. I'm already prepared to do that. You will see what I mean, soon enough." He smiled as he focused on me, then his boat moved away and he was gone.

One of the vulture women ordered me to get into Mrs. Cavan's boat, and then she climbed in, too. We docked at the barge, went up the stairs, then passed through a frigid corridor until we reached a vacant room where three ice sculptures stood. I approached cautiously. Both Mam's and Ishleen's statues were dark, a single tiny hole drilled into both their necks, and I assumed that was how their ghost souls had been drawn out. My entire being pulsed with remorse. It was because of my weakness that this had happened to them. I could hardly bear to imagine what each one was feeling, enclosed in the airless dark boxes. I stood before them, unable to leave.

"You should look at the third statue, Maeve," Mrs. Cavan said.

I glanced over. It was an ice sculpture of me.

I stared at it in shock. It was like looking in a mirror and seeing myself petrified and translucent. Clearly Tom had ordered it himself, because it wore an angry, defiant expression.

"That's what he meant, you know," Mrs. Cavan said. "Your ghost soul could easily be put into this. I've seen it done. It is an unbelievably simple process."

The vulture woman eyed me and smiled.

"Let's go," Mrs. Cavan demanded.

As we continued on, I saw some of the tundra girls peering at us from the frozen entrance of a corridor.

"Go away!" Mrs. Cavan cried, waving an arm in their direction. I noticed Breeze and the other ash girls with them, cleanly dressed for a change. It must have been the true fire that had helped them escape the basement dungeon, I thought.

I gave a meaningful look to Gudrun and Breeze, then said aloud as if to Mrs. Cavan, "Where are the black iron boxes with my mother and sister in them?"

"Do you really think I'd tell you?" Mrs. Cavan sneered.

She and the vulture woman led me into the vast room outside the chapel of the frozen mothers and tied my hands to two metal rings ensconced in the wall, then left, locking the door.

For a long time there was only silence. I fell into a shivering sleep.

I was swimming down, trying to find Danu's candelabra. I saw it burning very far below, naked men swimming around it. One of them clutched it beneath the burning candles, the flames waving slowly in the current. I saw his figure become slender and darker before it disappeared with the candelabra in an undulating swim.

I awakened suddenly. Gudrun and Breeze had come in. We listened closely to see if Uria was eavesdropping, but we could not feel the pulse of her heartbeat. "She has been listening obsessively to Mrs. Cavan and to Tom," Gudrun said, "and maybe even to the vulture women she might be suspicious of. She knows something is going on."

"How did you undo the lock?" I whispered

"With the flame," Breeze answered, moving aside her jacket and showing me a necklace with a bottle containing a vibrant red flame similar to the one the Swan Woman had given me years back. "Everything here on this barge softens and responds immediately to contact with true fire."

Breeze introduced the flames to the knots on the ropes around my hands, and they gave way quickly.

"Didn't they notice that you'd escaped the dungeon?" I asked Breeze as she and Gudrun worked hard to unravel the ropes.

"They pay so little attention to us, and think us of so little consequence," she answered. "And without blue ashes on us, we are no different from the others."

"And the vulture women," Gudrun said, "are so disorganized and so distracted because they are sure Tom Cavan will soon be coming into power. There are a few that are still unsure and are afraid to betray Uria. Those are the ones we watch out for more. They have more interest in what goes on here."

At last, I was completely untied. I rubbed my wrists and forearms, chafed and sore from the ropes.

"Do you know where the iron boxes are?" I asked.

"They're in Mrs. Cavan's room. She demanded tea before taking her nap. Trillip hid inside behind the curtain, crept about and watched until she found them hidden under the bed. She was going to try to take them then, but she must have made some noise, because Mrs. Cavan woke and sat up in her bed. Trillip managed to escape but without the boxes. At least we know where they are."

I told them about my meeting with Danu and how she'd instructed me to look for a druid wheel camouflaged among navigational equipment. "It has a triple spiral emblem forged on it," I said with quiet urgency. "If we can somehow loosen that wheel and let it release from its stuck position, time and vitality might return to the air of this barge. Every frozen soul will be released. The real fire will help us find it. Otherwise, the search will be difficult. False light will only keep it hidden."

"There are a few places on this barge with a lot of wheels and pipes," Breeze said.

"One place," I added, "is downstairs in the basement where you lived."

"Having spent seven centuries in that basement, I can guarantee you that there isn't one with a druid symbol."

"There are wheels and pipes in a room connected to the chapel of the frozen mothers," Gudrun said. "And a lot in the vestibule that leads to Uria's lair, guarded by the spiders and that other creature. But without a narcotic on the air current, it is too dangerous a place to go."

"Danu gave me something," I said. "This shawl is woven with true firelight and can even ignite without injuring me if I need it to. I will look in the vestibule, and you two go to the other room."

We crept quietly out into the corridor and to our respective places to search. At the threshold of the vestibule, I stepped into a shadow. I rubbed one of the beads on my shawl, and it glowed, illuminating everything around me in vague reddish light. There were dozens of defunct rust-encrusted wheels, warped wood pieces and metal pipes. The spiders with the women's faces stared at the red light, paralyzed. The chimera awakened and turned, looking wide-eyed at the redness, which soon faded. Feeling bold, I entered farther into the vestibule and was about to rub the bead again for another moment of light when I felt a succinct, powerful blow at the back of my neck and an explosion of astonishing pain. Everything faded to black.

CHAPTER 23

I awakened in a torrent of confusion, shaky and nauseated.

I turned toward a blur of brightness and focused until I saw a log burning false fire, and I thought for a moment that I was in the bedroom where I had stayed and the snow had fallen. My nerves began to prickle when something moved. On the floor, the fleshy cord snaked and slid, knotting and unknotting itself, winding and unwinding in a pile. Attached to it was Uria's emanation, bent over my shawl, examining it cautiously. Sensing I was awake, her head whipped around and she peered at me with her falcon eyes. The shawl was all that might protect me from her, and it was out of my reach.

The flesh walls around us began to breathe and contract.

The emanation did not move its mouth, the voice low

and booming and disembodied as she asked, "Weren't you told not to trespass here?"

"Yes, Goddess."

"What were you looking for?"

"I was looking for you, Goddess," I said.

She paused as if considering something, and then asked, "Where did you go when you left the barge?"

"I tried to escape. I've always hated Tom Cavan. His mother brought me here under false pretenses. I never wanted to marry him, Goddess. I tried to find the Holy Isles."

"Did you reach them?"

"No, but I saw one of Danu's servants, a Swan Woman. She sent me back here."

The emanation loomed suddenly very close, her golden eyes large and staring. But it was the cord of flesh that struck me as the more sentient part of Uria, quivering and attentive. The emanation at some moments looked like nothing more than a doll. The flesh cord brushed against my leg, and my nerves prickled cold, my body stiffening so intensely that I could not breathe. The shawl was too far away for me to reach.

Pit them against each other, I thought, remembering Danu's words.

"Tom has gone to retrieve a very valuable weapon, but he made me promise not to tell you."

The emanation deflated slightly for a moment, then swelled up, and the disembodied voice boomed, "Why are you telling me?"

"Because I hate him, Goddess. He has trapped my

mother's and sister's ghost souls in two black iron boxes. I have come to you to ask you to release them, and I will do anything for you."

The cord of flesh shivered, and traces of foaming saliva appeared at the corners of the emanation's mouth.

Her voice tolled like a low bell of doom as she asked, "Where has he gone to find the weapon?"

"This place," I said, my hand shaking as I reached into my pocket for the other map.

The emanation grabbed it, and her fleshy cord rose up in a high undulation, then slapped the ground like a heavy whip.

She held the map near the blue fire and studied it.

Something occurred to me. "His mother is also trying to help him. He wants to be a god, you see. He wants to usurp you."

For a moment, the fleshy cord itself seemed to disintegrate into particles. I remembered what Danu had said about anger weakening Uria, and I took it further. "Tom's mother is guarding my mother and sister in the iron boxes. It was originally her idea to betray you. He has also persuaded some of the vulture women. He says he will have the weapon soon and he will be a god."

The fleshy cord and emanation both began to shudder uncontrollably. Suddenly a deafening crack sounded from the other side of the lair, and I saw ice thawing and dripping at an unnatural rate. All I could assume was that the heat of Uria's rage was melting the cocoon. At the same instant, I heard ice howl and break outside from the barge, groaning as it crashed into the sea, its echoes causing the floor and walls to shudder.

I watched with awe as Uria's original body, releasing gusts of steam, broke free of the frozen bed. The ice frosting her hair and clothes melted and trickled away. She was more massive than the emanation, standing and struggling to move her limbs, still wounded with red and open sores that Danu had inflicted seven centuries before. The life went out of the emanation. It remained attached to her by the long cord, floating and bobbing above, like a balloon. Uria noticed the crystal apple in its cage of threads meant for the Fire Opal. She stared horrified at it, then tore it out and threw it against the wall, shattering it. She seemed, in her swollen fury, to have completely forgotten me.

Making a horrific noise and clutching the map, Uria moved heavily out of the lair. I grabbed the shawl, then followed as she stormed clumsily through the vestibule. The vulture women who were still true to her flanked and swarmed around her. I watched as she made her way through the corridors, groaning like the ice around her barge. In slow motion, and with a low-pitched, drawn-out roar, she ordered the barge steered south and inland toward Rosscoyne.

Uria knocked down the door of Mrs. Cavan's room and grabbed the sleeping woman by the hair, dragging her after.

When the boat was close enough to shore, the giant Uria walked across the rocks still dragging Tom's mother, who kept screaming out her son's name.

I ran out to one of the decks, where I found Gudrun, who handed me the shifts and veils meant for Mam and Ishleen. They folded up quite small, and I hid them in the pocket where I had carried the Fire Opal.

"All the girls have laid the ethereal dresses over the ice carvings of their mothers," she said excitedly. Then, eyes opening wide, she pointed out past my shoulder toward Ard Macha. The mist that usually encased the ice barge had broken up and dissipated, and from the decks where we stood, we could now see Uria climbing the hill to Rosscoyne. I told Gudrun that she should get a group of tundra and ash girls to help her unhinge the dormitory of their mothers' bodies and let it fall into the water. Just as she ran off to do this, I saw Wheeta.

"Get girls to help you prepare a group of small boats so everyone can flee into the surrounding water and wait there for their mothers' ghost souls in the dresses to float down to them!"

I rushed inside, back to the vestibule, where I breathed on my shawl. The garment ignited, and immediately I saw the triple spiral on a wheel glowing red in response to the fire. The spiders crouched in a back corner looking for refuge in a shadow.

The firelight illuminated the face of the chimera, and with a shock I recognized for the first time who he was: Michael Cavan, Tom's father.

"Mr. Cavan!" I said. "How did this happen?"

He looked sadly at me in his bizarre form. "I am too ashamed to say."

"You don't have to. I think I know, and I am very sorry for you."

I struggled to twist and turn the wheel from its locked position. "The awful magic is sustained here because of this wheel," I told him.

"Let me help you, Maeve," Mr. Cavan said.

In order to melt some of the ice, I rubbed a bead and held fire directly up to the wheel, so that the frost disintegrated and dripped away from it like a waterfall. When we tried to turn it again, it gave suddenly, with a great hissing exhalation accompanied by gusts of mist and condensation. The ice-locked walls began to dribble and steam, and release eerie, echoing screeches.

"Come with me," I said.

Encased in my shroud of red and orange flames, I moved through the corridors of rapidly melting ice. Through a big arch in the passageway, I saw the hull that comprised the dormitory of mothers adrift in the tide, and felt a pang of joyous satisfaction. In spite of the wetness everywhere, numerous self-contained fires broke out as I passed. Mr. Cavan followed closely after, breathing noisily, awkward on his four thin, stiff legs.

I got on the floor in Mrs. Cavan's room and searched under the bed, but the iron boxes were not there.

"Tom has put my mother's and sister's ghost souls into two iron boxes," I told Mr. Cavan. "I've got to find them."

He helped me search, tossing things aside, pulling drawers from bureaus and emptying them.

The fire was overtaking the corridors, and even Mrs. Cavan's room was now going up in flames. "We can't stay here, Maeve," Mr. Cavan said.

The smoke began to blind him and burn his eyes, and he gasped, choking for breath. I grabbed a folded blanket off the bed, and as I offered it to him to breathe through it to block the smoke, something fell to the floor: the two boxes.

"Mr. Cavan, I have them!" I cried out.

We rushed out the nearest open arch into the clearer air of the deck.

Most of the ancient ghost souls from the statues on the outer deck fled upward into the sky like startled herons, but some floated just above the dripping statues, then dispersed in the firelight.

A school of misbegotten mermaids, panicking at the chaos and disaster, swam in undulating trails into the distant water and disappeared beyond the mist. That's when, to my relief, I saw the tundra and ash girls standing in little boats on the water, drifting to a safe distance from the barge.

As their boats rose and dropped on the massive waves, the girls began singing "The Canticle of Fire," their arms open as they gazed upward. I braved the flames and ran to the entrance of the chapel of the frozen mothers. Looking in, the floors covered in melting ice, I saw clouds of light releasing from collapsing ice figures, wriggling and finding their way into the ethereal clothes. As the ghost souls streamed steadily out wearing their pale, glimmering ethereal shifts, they floated down upon their daughters, embracing them in particles and light.

Seeing this, I was flooded with hope. "Mam! Ishleen!" I said quietly to the boxes. "I'm going to see you both soon."

I looked toward Rosscoyne bog. Vultures were circling and screeching wildly, many of them departing in terror. I stood and bent into the wind, and it lifted me and carried me a few feet above the water until I reached the shore. I climbed the hill quickly and saw Tom and Uria facing each other at either side of the bog. Uria still had hold of Mrs. Cavan, who cried out now and again in pain. Tom stood tensely in a defensive posture, filthy with peat and bog water, while embers flew wildly around Uria.

"Get away from this bog, Tom Cavan!" Uria's demand boomed across the landscape.

"I won't," he shouted back.

"I have your mother here, and she will suffer if you do not go."

"I'm not going," he said matter-of-factly.

In a sudden fit of rage, Uria tossed Mrs. Cavan into the bog.

Tom reacted very little, only to take on an even more defensive stance, never taking his eyes off Uria.

Swans circled and screeched, slews of them coming in from the western sea along with herons and gulls. Falling feathers and floss met the fire around Uria, singeing to ash and floating away.

To my shock, the wind caught my skirts and lifted me high on the air. The shawl began to burn, so I was encircled in an aura of fire. The wind carried me until I was floating directly above Uria and Tom. Both looked up, in complete shock. Tom was too dumbfounded to move, while Uria grabbed for me several times. But the wind held me aloft just out of her reach. In her frustration, the skin of her face and arms began to blister and scorch.

"The ancient weapon, the Answerer, is not here in this bog," I called down to them. "Danu's return to Ard Macha is imminent."

"Maeve O'Tullagh!" Tom cried out. "You will suffer for this!" Seeing him so distracted and off his guard, Uria stepped across the bog, lifted Tom and hurled him into the peat where she'd thrown his mother. Sparks flew from her arm. Watching him sink, she fumed and her hair burst into a crown of fire.

Soon Uria's entire body was engulfed in flames. She stood with her arms raised, becoming less and less substantial, until all that was left of her was her spinal column, a massive blackened relic lying on the earth.

I was surprised by the pity I felt for Uria, blundering monster that she was, helpless against her own nature.

I descended slowly from the air, and the flames on my shawl went out. The iron boxes I held sprang their lids, and as Mam and Ishleen issued forth, I covered them immediately in the shifts and veils. They embraced me, two spangled, animated ghosts.

CHAPTER 24

The three of us, myself and the semitransparent figures of my mother and sister, waited awhile, watching the bog nervously lest Tom rise again.

I waved at the tundra and ash girls with their ghost mothers in the bay below. Their small boats had surrounded the dormitory with their mothers' bodies in it, which was afloat like an iceberg. Industrious creatures that they were, a group of the girls were working busily with a series of ropes, securing the dormitory to a system of boats which were clearly meant to pull it after. I imagined that they were preparing to sail back to their old latitudes in search of what was left of their culture.

During all the chaos, they had, it seemed, befriended Mr. Cavan, still in his awkward, monstrous form. He was on the boat with Breeze and Gudrun and their mothers. He waved up at me sadly.

I understood why he did not want to come back to Ard Macha.

Yet it seemed extreme that he would choose to go so far away, as if there were nothing at all left of his life. In his expression, I saw a fateful resignation. He turned away and faced the horizon to the north.

Old Peig was standing on the cliff watching the catastrophic fire on the water, and waved when she saw us coming.

I led the two shimmering figures to their bodies inside. Diligent Peig had wrapped them in shawls and set them comfortably before the hearth.

For a few prolonged moments, the ghost souls gazed in hesitant wonder at their inert forms and made quiet, pitying sounds. Ishleen was quicker than Mam to reenter her body. Her ghost soul sat on the body and embraced it, and as she disappeared into the flesh, the garment of ether fell and lay in a small heap in her lap. Ishleen blinked and twitched her fingers. Then, after taking a few seconds to focus her eyes, she smiled at us.

"You go now, Nuala," Old Peig urged.

"It's been so long." Mam's voice sounded on the air above us. "Where is Desmond? And where are my sons?"

"Still fighting the good cause, Nuala," Peig said. "But

word has come in that a big English fort has been destroyed and no rebels have been captured, so they are at large somewhere, being sheltered by good people."

Mam sighed, then reached over and touched the shoulder of her vacant body, looking at it wistfully like some long-lost sister. She moved near and embraced it, her ghost figure dissolving and the shift and veil falling to the floor.

Mam's hands moved first. Then her eyes opened. She sat forward slowly and uncertainly, and cried a little with relief.

"Listen to me, Mam and Ishleen. And you listen, too, Peig, so you know," I said. "Since you two were separated from your bodies, a thread has been broken. You might sometimes feel an urge to separate again for a few hours. If you do, you must always put on the ethereal shift and veil. That will keep you safe until you return to your bodies."

They listened to me thoughtfully and nodded gravely when I asked them if they understood.

As Peig stoked the fire, she said she would guard the ethereal clothes with her life. I hung them on pegs right near the box bed. In low light, they were so subtle that they almost became invisible, but as flames rose in the hearth fire, they twinkled, and when I looked closely at them, I could see them quiver.

"Maeve," Mam said, and reached for my hands, bringing them to her face and pressing her cheek against them. "Thank you, my daughter," she said, looking into my eyes. "You never gave up on me or on your sister. It's always been you I've felt there."

Old Peig gave Mam and Ishleen stew and tea, which they relished and sighed over. When they'd finished, Mam said, "My bones ache a bit. For now I just want to be near the fire."

Ishleen curled up on Mam's lap, and Peig added another brick of turf so that the flames sparked up high and hot.

When I looked closely at Ishleen in the firelight, I was amazed to see that she had small feathers at her hairline and, like the goddess, miniature feathers for eyelashes and eyebrows.

I overheard Mam weeping quietly. "Oh, missus," she whispered to Old Peig. "How I wish my husband was here. How I've longed to reconcile with him!"

My heart leapt. I heard Da say my mother's name, his voice low-pitched and soft. But it was only the wind moaning between the stones of the cottage wall.

While Mam and Ishleen slept, I told Old Peig about Mr. Cavan. "It surprised me that he left Ard Macha so completely. The tundra girls will likely be traveling a very long time to the distant places they lived centuries ago. He doesn't even know where he's going, only that he's going very far."

"The poor man," Old Peig said, and shook her ancient

head. "Tom probably cursed his father, and when a child casts a spell on his own parent, that spell is one that cannot be broken. Mr. Cavan must know that he is condemned to live the rest of his days in that unnatural form."

I went back to the loft area where my brothers used to sleep and looked at their things.

I took out *The Book of Invasions* and studied the battling figures in the etching on the first page. It made me sad to think that the female world and the male world in this house were so divided.

How I ached to tell Da and my brothers everything I'd done, about the journey I'd made to the Holy Isles and back. I imagined them listening, acknowledging me with their engrossed silence, their attentive eyes and occasional nods. I imagined them asking questions, wanting to know the nature of the weather or the night sky in the Other World. Somehow, I thought, our worlds could not be so far away from each other as they felt. But I did not think that it would be possible to tell them. They would not believe me and would call me Mad Maeve, as they had in the past, and I could not have borne for them to do that after everything I'd been through. No, I thought, that would be unbearable.

The thick, serious volume of *The Book of Invasions* made me feel lonely. I leafed through it, reading the names and dates of battles, the stark details of slaughter.

A dried fuchsia blossom, as delicate as paper, fluttered

loose of the book and fell to the floor. Da had given me this flower many years before, and I had placed it between these pages and forgotten about it. I suddenly missed Da deeply. I wanted him to see Mam, to speak to her. I wanted to see them embrace, the awful rift ended between them.

I was about to close the book when I found, marking another page, Fingal's drawings of the night sky from one June years before, when it had been very clear and he had been able to mark the movements of the stars the entire month. How carefully, how devotedly he had drawn and charted everything. I remembered him struggling for precision, looking at the sky with such intent, as if knowing somehow that it might help him understand our lives.

And then, in another section, I found something written in Donal's compact scrawl. *There are and always have been two realms existing simultaneously: the Everyday World and the subtler realm not everyone can perceive, known as the Other World. But each parallels and informs the other. Like the soul is to the body, the Other World is to the Everyday World.*

He had written it years ago, before he had begun to devote his entire self to the secret rebellion, when he'd still liked to imagine the Holy Isles and had insisted to Fingal that they were real. Even though he'd changed since then, Donal had the romantic nature of a poet. If anyone might listen, maybe it would be Donal.

I took heart, and lay down exhausted in my bed.

* * *

I was following a trail of dead birds. They led me to Tom Cavan, who was bent over a heap of kelp on the beach. I approached. The Answerer, with its penetrating eye, lay there like another of Tom's victims, its jewel eye cracked and clouded. Tom turned to me with a cruel smile.

I awakened gasping. Shaking, I got up and checked on Mam and Ishleen and Old Peig. The ethereal shifts glimmered calmly on their pegs. I tried to reassure myself. The Answerer, according to Danu, was still safely hidden in the buried room, and Uria was now conquered. But at that hour, as everyone slept, I heard a distinct unease in the wind and the sea, the surf turning anxiously upon itself. Some darkness still held Ard Macha in its thrall.

I feared, in my twilight mind, that maybe Tom would find a way to survive, thriving on mud and mineral and rot, then emerge somehow from the bog. I went outside and took a deep breath, trying to put that thought to rest, reassuring myself that it was only a dream, and remembered what Danu had said about the nature of the Rosscoyne bog.

I was about to go back in when I felt a stirring on the air, and thought of Francisco. He had eluded death by sea and death by English bullets. He had eluded Uria's henchwomen and Uria herself.

I heard, very faintly, so that I was not sure if it was real or hallucination, strains of "The Canticle of Fire."

Looking south to the rocks along the headland, I saw light near the water's edge. I went down in the cold wind, clutching my shawl tight around me, and as I descended, I saw Danu's candelabra, the tide foaming up and splashing the rock it sat on. My heart went wild. I could not help but relate its presence here to Francisco, and remembered the vague figures of human males in my dream, swimming on the seafloor around it.

I moved closer. The candelabra lit the water in its proximity, so I seemed to see things in the twisting tide. Kelp tended to look like fabric, and with an almost painful anticipation, I was certain that I was about to see a deluged Spanish jacket, its silver embellishment issuing steam. But the water shifted, and there was no jacket.

I stayed watching the water, waiting for it to leave something in the damp around the rocks, but it kept touching them and retreating, leaving nothing behind. Lifting my eyes to the dark distances of the horizon, I wondered where Francisco was this very hour.

ACKNOWLEDGMENTS

Deep gratitude goes to my husband, Neil, and daughter, Miranda, for invaluable support, love and a lot of laughter! Much thanks to Claudia Gabel for inviting me to write for young adults; to Françoise Bui for important feedback and for taking this book through the many editorial stages to publication; and to the sharp eyes of copy editors Ashley Mason and Bara MacNeill. Gratitude to my agent, Joy Harris, and also to Adam Reed and Jodi Keller. Love and thanks to Daniel Chausow and Nina Chausow for help with translations into Spanish, and to Diane Garrett of Diane's Books, for generosity, friendship and her unshakable devotion to the Queendom of the Imagination.

ABOUT THE AUTHOR

Regina McBride is the critically acclaimed author of three novels for adults: *The Marriage Bed, The Land of Women,* and *The Nature of Water and Air. The Fire Opal* is her first book for young adults. The winner of fellowships from the National Endowment for the Arts and the New York Foundation for the Arts, she teaches creative writing at Hunter College in New York City, where she lives with her husband and daughter.